JUST
MATES

John Gumbs

Published by John Gumbs
Publishing partner: Paragon Publishing, Rothersthorpe
First published 2020
© John Gumbs 2020, London

ISBN 978-1-78222-751-9

Book design, layout and production management by Into Print
www. intoprint.net
+44 (0)1604 832149

Contents

Chapters

In this chapter I meet up with two chaps from Nottingham.
We worked together at the railyard cleaning trains. From that
moment on we kept together, along with our girlfriends.

1

In the Nottingham rail yard

Nottingham was a small settlement a long time ago around the 6th century. It was a Saxon village. It had the name of *Snotta Inga Ham*. The real meaning was that the village was owned by Snotta.

Later, it changed to Snottingham.

The Danes when they came over and took England, Nottingham became a fortified place for them. Later the king of England took it back and built a bridge across the Trent. Around the 10th century Nottingham was a very busy town. William the Conqueror built a castle all of wood for the safety of Nottingham. In the 12th century it was built with stone.

In 1155 Nottingham got a charter from the king; its first Mayor in 1284; and its first Sheriff in 1449. There was a market and an annual fair. In the 13th century friars came to Nottingham. There was also a jewish community; but later, all the Jews had to leave England in 1290. There was also Sherwood Forest, a big thick area of wood where it was almost impossible to penetrate through.

Robin Hood lived in this forest.

A grammar school was later founded in 1513. Outside the gate of Nottingham were two leper hostels, they were closed down by Henry VIII. Walton Hall was erected by Robert Smythson in 1588.

•

I came down from London in 1961 and took up residence at Nottingham. I was living about 300 metres away from the main station. Across the road over the bridge was the railway yard where all the dirty trains came in to be cleaned from all the mud and muck that they had picked up either on the main line or on short journeys between towns.

My name is Jarvis Granville and I worked at the railway yard as a cleaner. It is the month of April and I'm on the first shift along with my other two mates, Terry and Bill – both as nutty as a fruit cake, but trustworthy and honest. As we came into the entrance of the yard with the office on the left and clock-in system right, there by the window, Terry said with a grin,

"That chick in the office, I'd do anything to go out on a date with her."

"Why don't you ask her?" I said. "You never know your luck!"

"Look at me, man, do you think she'll have someone like me?"

"You look ok to me, I don't see anything wrong with you," I told him. "You'll never know until you try."

"Now someone like you have more luck, even though you're black! No offence eh!"

"It's ok! I know what you mean!"

When we got to the window, one of the two girls whose name was Jane said, *"Surprise! Surprise!"*

"What you talking about?" I said to her. "Have you made up your mind at last to surprise me?" Many times I had tried to get her to go out with me.

"In your dreams," she said, and carried on looking at papers.

We clocked in and went to the main hangar. I stopped suddenly as I looked at the turn-table. There was a green train there on it. It was really black and greasy and mucky. I saw patches of green here and there. The other two chaps stopped as well. Bill said, "I don't believe it. Are my eyes playing tricks on me? This is a *master* train! By God we're lucky!"

"It's still a dirty train, what is lucky about that? Maybe, that's why Jane said 'surprise, surprise.'"

After meeting the foreman and other workers, we went and had a closer look. I saw the writing on the train, it said: **Flying Scotsman**. I remembered reading about this train. It was built in Doncaster. It started out in 1923 with the number 1472; later it was changed to 4472. It had its first non-stop service from London to Edinburgh.

"This train," I said to my co-workers, "was the first train to do 100 mph in the UK."

Terry said, "Let's get started and get all the filth off of it."

"After we're finished with it, we all be black as soot," I remarked.

Terry and Bill started laughing. They found what I had said very funny.

Bill said: "And when it is there in all its glory, green as ever and sparkling, we know we have done a good job."

"What you talking about?" Terry came in. "We *always* do a good job on the trains that come into the yard."

"I tell you what I will do," I said, "I will ask Jane again to go out with me."

"Some luck there my friend," Bill told me. "She's going to turn you down. She doesn't look the type who wants a boyfriend. She's the homely, mummy and daddy type."

"You could be wrong," I told him. "Well, I'll still try anyway."

Cleaning steam trains is really a dirty job. But it's interesting. We learn quite a lot about how the trains tick; and how the whole Railway System works. If we work hard we can get promoted to fireman and then as driver. To become a fireman is very important, and we have to look after the fire that makes the engine run, through steam. This is a great task and one has to be very skilful. Sometimes we have to couple the train to the carriages, and be alert for rail signals.

It took us a few hours before we had the *Flying Scotsman* as spanking new. There it was on the turn-table – gleaming. We were proud of ourselves and gave each other a pat on the back. Later, when we were checking out to go home, I said to Jane, "There's a good movie on at the flicks, would you like to go?"

"Maybe," she said softly.

"Everything's on me."

"Well, okay, pick me up at 8 pm."

"I will do just that," I told her, feeling pleased with myself because she accepted my date.

Bill said that he will come along with his girlfriend.

Terry wasn't sure as yet, he was still looking to find himself a steady girl.

"It can't be that hard to find a girl," I told Terry. "The girls here in Nottingham outnumber the men five to one."

"I know!" he replied. "I just hadn't given it a try."

We made arrangements and then we all went to our homes. At 8 pm sharp I went to Jane's home, and from there we went to our usual cafe where we met up with the others. Bill introduced his girlfriend and we sat down for a milk-shake.

"Now I know what that 'surprise' was," I said to Jane. "It really was a great surprise."

"Yeah!" Bill said. "We've never had such a train like that before, and it's the nation's most famous train."

Terry said, "It was a real pleasure cleaning it. What a great treat that was!"

Jane said, "When the papers came into the office, I was thinking of you boys and how pleased you would be when you saw it. A real special one."

After our milk-shakes we left and went to the flicks. The film was *LA DOLCE VITA*, a comedy, very funny. We never saw all of the film at all. Jane and I did nothing but cuddling and kissing. Bill was doing just the same. Poor Terry had to do with being alone, with no one to kiss or cuddle, still, he didn't mind. One day, he'll get his own girl. When the film ended, and we had eaten our popcorn and ice creams, we went out and had fish and chips.

A week later we all went to watch Forest lose to Bolton Wanderers. In this League division one match at Burnden Park, Forest did not play well at all. Still, as fans, we enjoyed the match – and the day out. The following week at City Ground, we saw Forest draw with Leicester City – a delightful match. This is the match that Terry should never ever forget because it was here that he met his girlfriend, Trisha.

She was a brunette, very elegant, good company to be with, and had a strong sense of humour. So we all now had our own girfriends, and weren't jealous of each other. As a group of six, we did things together; went to dances; cricket matches; footbal matches; hockey matches; tennis matches and all the other sports that came around. Trisha had a job in the Midland Bank and Bill's girfirend was a secretary to a lawyer in the city. Her name was Susan and she was a blonde with blue eyes, nice figure, pleasant company.

Terry and Bill always wore pointed shoes and a black jacket full of silver studs – you know, like Teddy Boys wore. I don't know if they were real Teddy Boys, but they acted rough at times, were decent in many ways. If we had to go to a do, where we had to dress up, they would wear a sort of suit with a thin tie like shoe-string. I wasn't a Teddy Boy but I didn't mind being with them.

I shall tell you how I came to be friends with Terry and Bill.

One day all three of us had been working on a coal heap, at back of yard. I was new then, and Terry tried to take advantage of me, because I was black, but I showed him a thing or two by not backing down. Bill was really surprised when I tackled Terry, and we both fell in the coal, blackened faces with dust all around. I knew I had to avoid being kicked, so I tackled the legs very hard so that he found it difficult to manoeuvre. That was when Bill made his move to try and stop me from overpowering his mate. I held on to both of them as we wrestled in the coal dust. It was then that the foreman came and stopped us from killing each other. Our blue coveralls were blackened from the coal dust, and both Terry and Bill had blackened faces. Later, we had to go into the office and explain ourselves. From that moment onwards, Terry, Bill and I became mates. And if any other person tried to bother me, Terry and Bill would step in.

I remember once we were at Bill's place, and the whole living room floor was covered with 45 singles. We were all really mad on music. Always waiting for the new releases. There was a time too when all six of us were kicked out of our front seats in the flicks because we were making too much noise, gigling and playing around as if we were outside. We were only kids all of us just turning 18.

There was another time when we went to the annual goose fair. We really did enjoy ourselves. The grounds where this is held – The Forest Recreation Ground – has quite a number of attractions. We all let ourselves go, enjoying the rides and the food and just having a good time. At the end of it we were all shattered and needed about a week's rest.

Things were going well for all of us until Bill came up with idea of joining the army. The girls weren't pleased when they heard of it.

2

Holidays & joining the army

Back at work, the *Flying Scotsman* has gone and we are back with the normal trains. Now and then, we would go out on a train to Derby, Beeston, Long Eaton, and many other places. But most of the time, we were in the yard and cleaning the trains. We did other jobs as well around the yard.

All six of us were in our usual cafe one day when Terry came up with the idea of going over to the continent.

I said, "That's a good idea, we could go to Germany, and pop over the border to Holland."

The girls were all pleased about it and just couldn't wait for it to happen.

Bill said, "Ok then, that's settled! Make sure that everyone has a passport and ID."

Terry said, "We shall go for two weeks, it will do us all good."

That summer, we left on a plane from Heathrow to Schiphol.

It was a lousy day when we arrived. We stayed in and played cards. The following days were good with plenty of sunshine. There were many things to see, many places to go to. We ended up on a beach at a place called Scheveningen for two days, very enjoyable. You always find that when you're on holidays, the days just fly past. Well, it was so with us.

We were back in Nottingham, and back on our jobs.

One evening at the flicks, Bill told us something that had Terry and I really thinking. He suggested that all three of us join the army.

I said, "No way! That's giving up our freedom."

Terry said, "We're still young, and doing that for three years at least would give us some extra experience."

"What about our girlfriends?" I told him. "We'd only see them sometimes at the weekend, and then there's the period when we won't see them for a very long time. I think we need to think about it much deeper."

Bill said, "The recruiting office is not far away. We can go and have a look."

The girls didn't say much on the subject but you could see that they weren't pleased. They let us decide for ourselves what we think was best for all of us. We finally decide that we should go and check the recruiting office out. See what they have to offer.

There was a tall man in the office with a well trimmed moustache. There were a couple others with him – all in uniforms. They greeted us very politely and listened to what we had to say. I made the case clear: we would only join the army if all three of us could be posted in the same regiment. The man said that that was no problem, and it would be done for us. We filled out some forms, did an IQ test, and he let us know that we'll all be sent to a special place for a medical check up. He gave us the dates, we thanked him and left.

Outside the office, I said to Terry and Bill, "It's that stupid poster that we see all around the town with that man on it saying, "The Army wants you."

Terry said, "You know, I was just thinking we might as well go and serve the country for three years. Then when we come back out, we would feel good knowing that we did our duty for Queen and country."

Bill said, "It wouldn't surprise me that as soon as we put the uniform on, war breaks out."

I whispered something in Terry's ear.

Bill said, "What was that?' What did you tell Terry that you didn't want me to know?"

I said, "It's a little secret. Terry will tell you later."

"Oh!"

*

A couple of weeks later, a letter came explaining what we had to do and where we had to go for the medical. After we had done all that, we were notified again that everything was ok, and that dates would be given to us after to report to the training regiment.

We had a get-together at our usual cafe; the girls were there. We knew the dates when we were to report to the training camp. This was to be our last week in Nottingham before we were on our way to Yorkshire where the camp was situated. I had read a lot on the history of Yorkshire. So I said: "Do you know that long ago, way back in ancient times, stone age hunters arrived in the area now known as Yorkshire?"

Trisha said, "I've had reading in history, especially British history. The whole place that you are talking about was completely covered with forests, and it was these farmers who started cutting down the trees, to make a way for farming."

"Yes," I said, "the Celts were also responsible for they were in Yorkshire after 500 BC. They had iron tools and weapons. There was a great tribe called the Brigantes and their capital was situated at a place called Aldborough."

Trisha tasted her milkshake then said: "The Romans arrived in South east England in 43 AD. They took over Eastern Yorkshire in 71 AD."

"Yorkshire is full of history like when the King of Norway, Harald Hardrada invaded England and sailed along the Humber and the Ouse. Then the Duke of Normandy won the battle of Hastings and became King of England. The people of Yorkshire in 1068 rose in rebellion. William marched his forces to York and built a fort there. When he left in 1069, the North rose in rebellion again.

William's men burned all the stores of food and the crops in the fields. They killed all the domestic animals and destroyed the farm tools. Many people there starved to death," I told them.

Bill said, "We're living in a time where we do not have to starve to death. There's an abundance of food everywhere. I know that where we're going, in the army, we will never starve."

Trisha said: "And what's the difference between *war of the roses* and *The war of the roses*?"

"The war of the roses," I said to her, "were the civil wars in the 15th century. War of the roses had to do with the struggle between Lancashire and York. Lancashire had the red rose while York had the white one."

Susan said: "It will be pleasant to come and visit you all there in Yorshire. My Bill will be first out the gate when I arrive."

Bill gave a smile and then looked at me. "Have we got time for a late movie?"

I said, "Yes." Then we all left the cafe and headed to the flicks.

It was one of those films, slow and dreary. Not one of us enjoyed it, but it was nice to be there with your girl.

On our night shift at the rail yard, we were back cleaning the same old trains. Nothing special came in. Terry said while we were in the tea room, "Soon we'll be off and leaving all this behind, showing off our beautiful uniform."

"That's right," I told him, "but it's best to show it off to our girls."

"You're right," he said, as he poured the cups of tea. Bill said that he was feeling a bit jumpy and nervous as the date for our departure drew near. After our shift was finished in the early hours of the morning, we clocked out and went to our homes.

*

The letters arrived early on a Monday. We had passed our medical with flying colours. The date was there and it was the end of the month. The following day we all met – the boys only because the girls had to work – and we thrashed out a few things. Now we were ready and prepared.

"Here we come, Yorkshire," I blurted out. "Here we come Royal Signals."

So we drank a few milk-shakes, and then planned our last days in Nottingham.

We had a reception at the rail yard with all the workers there. We had one at our usual cafe, and the last and final one, we had at Bill's home. We had our dates set to depart from Midland station.

We made sure that everything was ok, and that we knew all the train timings, and where to change. When all the celebrations were over, and all the kissing and hugging, and goodbyes were made, the six of us found ourselves on the platform and waiting for the train. Our suitcases were crammed pack with stuff and all sort of things that would come in handy for us.

The train came in on time. We had our last kisses and hugs and waves. We boarded the train. Inside I got to a window and opened it. Jane stood below on the platform.

"Don't forget to write," she said. "I know you'll be very busy when you get up there, but keep me in mind."

Terry and his girl were chatting away and I thought she was going to take the whole train back home with her the way she was holding on to the door. Bill and his girl were also busy saying last goodbyes, until the whistle blew and the train started moving slowly forward.

It went through the road tunnel moving faster now and leaving the station far behind. On the left side, as we looked out, was the railway yard. We all waved goodbye to it. We settled down and started playing some card games to pass the time away.

Forgetting to change trains, we stayed on the same train and ended up in the wrong destination. We finally

17

got to our training camp well after midnight. The Orderly corporal was there at the guardroom, and he saw to it we were fixed up with accomodation.

I must really say that the breakfast next morning went down well, but I wasn't pleased at all in the way how they woke us up. There were shouting saying, "Come on, let's have you up and ready..."

This went on for some time. We still got up in our own time when all the shouting had died down. After breakfast, still in the clothes that we came up in, we went to the quartermaster's store to be fully kitted out. When we got there, I said to the other two, "This is it, lads. This is the moment we have all waited for." We entered and started getting measured up for the uniforms.

The black boots were handed over the polished counter.

Bill said, "Did you see that ?"

"What?" Terry and I spoke at the same time.

Bill carried on, "Those boots on the quartermaster's feet? You can see your face in them."

We started getting all the items a soldier would need while he is in basic training.

A typical day is: waking up, make up your bed, clean yourself, clean your room, do outside areas, and have a room inspection. Parade for breakfast. Parade for lessons like field skills, rifle lessons, physical training, navigation, laws of armed conflict; battle field casualty drills; then drill quite a lot. Parade for lunch. Parade for more lessons; parade for end of work, usually around 5-6 pm; clean your kit; clean your room, and then go to bed.

We got a helmet with a camouflage net, webbing with pouches left and right; dress uniform, and ordinary working clothes in green. Socks, vests, undies in khaki and green along with other items.

When we were finally kitted out and back in our room, which had six beds in it – three on the right – and three on the left, we started packing neatly on the shelves in the long steel locker. Beside our beds was a small wooden locker, with about three drawers. That was it. There was nothing else in the room except a sizeable trash can and a board over a table where notices were placed. We were told that we had to report to a certain building where we would get more briefing. We went immediately to that place.

We got all the information that was available for the 14 weeks course. At least we learned that in the 7th week, families could come and visit. Later, we would also leave camp for a two week course to be held in the Lake District.

Back in the room on our beds, taking a little rest, Terry said: "It's only 14 weeks, this course, if we pull along and behave ourselves, we would get through it easily."

I said: "That's exactly what we're going to do. We're going to come out of this together, just like we've always done. The course is easy but it can appear as being hard if we take the wrong attitude."

Bill said, "The girls can come and visit after the 7 weeks are up."

I said, "They'd like that. You know, like what we used to do when we were back in Nottingham. A nice cafe, with milk-shakes and that sort of thing."

It was time to go for dinner which started at 17.00 hrs. The dining hall was packed but we managed to get to a table that was free. The food was really good. There was a lot on offer; so we sat down and tucked in. When dinner was finished, we left, took a slow walk around to see where things were situated such as the amenities building, swimming pool, tennis courts, and football fields.

Around 20.00 hrs, we went to the NAAFI canteen, had a drink and a game of darts. We made friends with a couple of other soldiers who were recruits like ourselves. I think one of them was from Dundee in Scotland, and the other was from Newcastle Upon Tyne.

The next morning we were in PT kit ready for our six miles run. Then after that shower, change, and breakfast. We were now getting used to the routine, and after a few six miles run every morning, we began to feel like Tarzan – strong, agile and extremely fit. We had to admit that this army life was changing us completely from civilian life. At Nottingham, when we finished working, we could do whatever we wanted to do. But here in the army, we could not do the same. Still, we found it exciting and challenging. We were only but young kids in a new adventure, and it was proving to be a positive one.

We had been down a few weekends by bus and rail to Nottingham where we took the girls out to the flicks and up to the dancing place.

Back in camp, the drill on the square was hard. We had to do a certain drill over and over again until the whole squad got it right together. We had lots of laugh to go with it as well. I remember one day, as we lined up on the square, the drill corporal instructor stood in the front. He shouted out the order very loud, and I saw how he twisted his mouth, and the spittle at the lips. I burst out laughing loud along with some others. He came right up to me, with his nose almost touching mine. He said:

"Do you find it funny, soldier? Fall out!"

I turned to my right, slammed my foot into position, and came out of the ranks. Then the corporal came right behind me, saying, "To the guardroom, left right, left right!" I marched off, and when we came to the guardroom, which was only about 150 metres away, there was no one there. He turned and said to me, "You're lucky." He told me to go back and fall in with the others, while he went to the phone in the guardroom office.

There were no more strange incidents during the rest of the drill operations. Everything went well. Families day came and the girls and us enjoyed ourselves. Then came the two weeks course in the Lake District area.

It was freezing cold then and most of the lakes were almost frozen over. We set up tents not far from a lake. The following morning we saw ice inside the roof of the canvas. On another day we had to go climb mountains with a pack on our backs. The mountains were very high, and there was a time when we were up high on one of them. We had to make our way across a small ledge which was very dangerous. It was very deep below us and we were told not to look down, but some of us did. We had to edge our way slowly across this ledge with our backs pressing hard into the mountain, and our hands – both of them – stretched out at the sides and digging into the earth, in order to stop us from falling off the ledge. Then we finally made it across with no casualties. We looked across and saw another mountain in the distance just about as high as the one we were on. The corporal in charge said that when we get off this mountain, we would climb that other one. You should have seen the faces then – not very pleased at all. We all got through, as tough as it was, we climbed the next mountain and made it back to our base camp. Some of us, later, actually went down to the lake, broke the ice and went in for a quick dip. I said a *quick* dip because it wasn't a real good thing to stay too long in that ice cold lake. Even some of the tough ones admitted that it was foolish to do so. We had something nice and hot to drink. I am now talking about army stew, you just can't beat it. It is great along with your bread and mug of tea.

*

After two weeks in the Lake District, we found ourselves back at the training camp. Terry, Bill and I phoned down to Nottingham to let them know what we had been through. A couple of weeks later, it was time for *pass off* parade. Here, we all dressed up in our best uniforms with the families and friends watching. We gave them a good old show. When it was all over, everyone was delighted. As for me, I had no one who came to pass off except Jane. My dad was in Nottingham. He had no interest in the army whatsoever, and it was he who had tried to stop me from joining up. He was furious about it. Another thing, he didn't like me going out with Jane.

Terry and Bill's families were there to watch the pass off parade. Even the girls came up as well. Jane and I later broke up, but still saw each other now and then. Terry and Bill and Trisha and Susan all found it sad, but there was nothing no one could have done to make it better. That was the way life went, and one had to be wise and accept the circumstances, one had to move on.

The weekend over, Terry, Bill and myself went back to our training camp. Later, we saw on the notice board all the postings. Many of us crowded around to get a good look and a read. I saw my name in a group for Germany. Just below, in another group, I picked out Terry and Bill's names, both for Germany. I was glad when I saw that they had the same regiment as myself. We left and went to the canteen and had a drink or two to celebrate. The drinks we had weren't alcohol, for I hadn't yet started drinking strong drinks.

After finishing training camp, all three of us – Terry, Bill and myself – got posted to the same regiment in Germany, not far from the Dutch border.

3

Germany, Holland

We had two weeks leave before we had to finally report to our overseas regiment. There was a date written down, and the time when we had to catch the plane that would take us over to Germany. I was all excited and could not wait for the day to arrive. I was told it would be best to start by learning a little bit of the language. I could not speak English well much more to take on another one – and German at that! I had read a lot and had seen many films about Germany – especially lots of war films. I was now thinking about all those soldiers who gave their lives for us to live. Now it is my turn to do something about it should another war break out. I was also thinking that I am now going over not to hate the Germans, but to try and live with them in peace. As far as I was concerned, it was all now in the past, and what had happened is now history. So I prepared myself with good intentions to be a good soldier and be respectful to the people in that country.

*

We arrived in good time to book in and board the plane. The journey took about an hour. When we arrived at the airport in Germany, we still had to get transport to take us to our camp, which was there and waiting.

We arrived at our working regiment at exactly midnight, and we were put into transit accomodation.

Terry said, "I feel like it's going to be ok here."

"Do you mean the regiment as a whole or this block?" I asked.

"The regiment... I'm... yes, I feel that it's very big," he told me.

"Can't wait till tomorrow," Bill said, "to see where they're going to put us."

The next morning we were taken to our final accomodation, H formed buildings right down at the back, next to the fence, and next to a wooded area. Our room in this H block was on the bottom floor with six beds in it. Each bed had beside it a tall steel locker, and a small wooden side locker. There was a table on the right side as we went through the swing doors. Over the table was a board where notices were placed.

We learned that one of the soldiers in the room was doing National service. He had not long to do now. We crowded around his bed and listened to some of his stories:

National service started in 1947 and soldiers who were 18 and healthy were allowed to sign up for 19 months. Later, it was raised to two years. This soldier whose name was Horace was tall, with a slim fit figure. He told us that some of the young ones didn't like the idea of National service. It caused a lot of violence, and some of them just didn't take to drills and bayonet practice. It was the corporals who were in charge.

"And you," I said, "you haven't got much time left!"

Horace said, "Just about three months, and I'll be leaving all this behind me. You regulars, you're committed. You have to sign on for three years, and if you like it, you can sign on for longer."

Terry said, "We're young, and I think it's good to be able to do this for ourselves and for the country. All soldiers, in any country, are protectors of the people. We get the chance too, to move around and see other countries."

Bill said, "After three years, I may actually sign on for another three, who knows?"

"Do not get me wrong," Horace said, "it's not all that bad. National service has its positive side. But not every one takes a liking to it." He then took a map from his locker, took us over to the table, opened the map, and pointed to where we were, then to the Dutch border. He said: "The Dutch border is here," pointing to a spot on the map. "To get there we would have to walk for at least 20-30 minutes. You can also order a taxi from the guardroom, at the head of the camp. The taxi is expensive, so we normally take the walk."

I said, "It's not very far at all, we can take a slow walk and get there."

"Of course, you can," Horace told me. "We have walked it many times. A group of us normally do the walk, sometimes only two of us. When you leave the camp, you will come to a farmer's village, a small one with a couple of shops. From there the road takes you through woods until you come to a place called 'Well', then you'll see the signposts showing directions to other places. The town of

Nijmegen is on the right and Venlo is on the left. There are other places in between."

Bill said, "That information is first class for we are going to need it when we start checking things and places out."

I said, "I saw a small village just before we got to our camp. Is anything there?"

Horace said, "There's a large pub with a garage at the back. It's pretty busy almost every night."

Terry said, "We'll check that out as well."

We had talks with another soldier who had a bed in our room. He was slim, not too tall, said he came from Cardiff. We called him Taffy because anyone who is from Wales is called by that name. He gave us lots of information on where we could go. Around 19.00 hrs all the chaps in the room decided to go to the Naafi fo a drink. I was already in bed and they all found it funny. They came and threw me out of bed, opened the window and threw the bedding outside.

"*Ok! Ok!* I'll come," I said. "But I'm not going to have any heavy drink."

Some of the lads went outside, around the block, and came to the middle part. They handed the bedding through the window. Then we all went to the Naafi bar. There was a canteen next door with a games room joined to it. In the bar there was a darts board, and we were lucky, for no one was playing on it. The chaps ordered their drinks and I was surprised to find Terry and Bill on the beer.

I said, "Give me half and half" (half beer, half lemonade).

"Still a kid, eh!" Terry said. "It's time to try something new."

We went over to the darts board and started playing

amongst ourselves. After a couple of those half and half, I was feeling strange, dizzy, felt like I wanted to throw up, and was saying, "That's it. No more of that stuff."

The guys said, "Most of what you had was shandy – women's drink, the rest was a little beer."

I said, "That wasn't little, it knocked me out. I'll have to take it slow from now on."

I said goodnight to all and went to bed.

On Monday morning at 08.00 hrs we were all there on parade in our working kit. We got inspected after the roll call, then we were given tasks to do. This went on like that everyday. At the weekend we were all free to do as we like. We checked out the village nearest to the camp. One day we were at the back where the garage is situated, and we saw a transaction taking place. A young chap had come to pick up his car, a white car that looked brand new. When he opened up the bonnet, he found there was no engine to be seen. We said to him, "Why did you not check it completely when you first came?" He was upset, we could see, and we left them there to sort that mess out.

We checked out other nearby places around the camp, but didn't find what we were looking for. The next weekend we went through the back fence, and started making our way to the Dutch border. Horace and Taffy came along.

We stayed around the area of Well, had a few drinks in the local bar, chatted with the barmaid, who seemed as if she had an interest in me.

Bill said, "There you go. She likes you."

I said, "I'm not going to rush in too quickly, just in case Jane and I could get back together."

Terry said, "You know that your father won't have it,

so there's no chance at all there for you. And anyway, Jane probably has another boyfriend."

It was getting late in the afternoon so we decided if we make a slow walk back, we could get in just in time for dinner. They all agreed and we started walking back. We got back in good time. We went to dinner, enjoyed it, and then went and relaxed on our beds.

Terry said: "That girl down at the border has eyes for you. Anyone can see that. We shall go back down there a few more times, you never know."

I said, "Take it easy, we'll see as time goes by. I don't want to make a fool of myself."

Bill said, "The walk down there was a long one but it was worth it. The border should have been much closer. They weren't thinking about us when they marked it off. Anyway, we can't do anything about it. Those Dutch people though, are very friendly."

"So are the German people," I said, "and they had once been our enemies. They treat us well, their hospitality is great."

Horace said, "Give me good old Scotland any time, a bite of haggis, and a glass of whisky."

"Still," I said, "it's good to be visiting other countries and learn their way of life."

*

The following month we left camp and went on an exercise for four weeks. It was a terrible winter. The cold sunk into us trying to tear us apart. There was a time when a massive tree fell on the roof of our 3-ton wagon. There were only four of us at that time. All the rest had gone in advance. We managed to clear the tree away, made our way slowly across dangerous ground, and finally got to where the advance party were stationed. It was late at night when we came in. We could hardly see anything. All the vehicles camouflaged among the trees, were hard to be spotted from above, and even from a distance along the ground. We went straight to the cook tent and had ourselves something hot to drink. We made sure our vehicles were safe and out of sight, then we crawled into our sleeping bags fully dressed just in case we were woken up in some sort of alert. There were quite a number of these alerts that had us really going.

The main one was gas alert. We had to put on a special kit along with our gas mask, and carry out normal work. Thank God that one didn't come around just yet. We could relax a bit.

I remember once back at camp, we all had to go into a building in gas mask kit, and carrying our gas masks. Inside it was a bit dark and weird. The corporal said, "Everything's going to be ok. It's not going to last long."

Suddenly, he threw something down on the floor, and we all immediately grabbed our gas masks which was hanging over our right shoulder. I saw one chap as he took his gas mask out of the pouch, it fell out of his hand, and onto the floor; he panicked for a while but was helped by others. The gas came at me, I was choking, eyes watering continuously. I managed to get my gas mask on. Then the door was opened. I rushed towards it. When I got outside, I grabbed the gas mask from my face, not caring if my face had come off as well, then I lifted my head up to the sky, and into the wind. What a relief that was! The wind lashed against my face and the breathing came back as normal. I placed the mask back into the pouch, and then went away with the group.

Back in camp after the exercise was over, we started planning to make a trip to Amsterdam. Everyone had been talking about it and saying that we had to go and see it ourselves. At the weekend we ended up at the bar, over the border in Well. We stayed there for some time. I had to get back to camp pretty sharp because I was on guard duty. Yes, I got used to that guard duty business. If your name is not on the board for duty, you had better get yourself away, and from the sleepimg quarters before some orderly corporal or sergeant came and suddenly inform you that you were on guard duty now. Someone whose name was on the list hadn't turned up or hadn't come back from leave.

*

Becuse we like football so much, Terry, Bill and I arranged a match for every Sunday morning among the soldiers who were still around. I remember one Sunday morning, it was pouring down with rain and the pitch was soggy. The goal areas were like a pig-sty, and yet there we were playing football ferociously. I was completely soaked and played as goalkeeper. I looked worse than the pigs when they have been rooting in the mud. We won the game anyway, and went back to the block, and to the showers.

Inside the showers, I heard someone say, "Come guys and have a look at this!"

We left our showers and went and had a look to see what was going on. There was this young soldier with the others around him, saying, "There's nothing there. How are you going to cope with those German girls? That is too small."

I said, "Leave the lad alone, he's a good soldier and very helpful. Wait until one of you are not feeling well, he'll be there to help you. Some of us has big ones and some of us has small ones. That is not what makes a man."

After the showers, we relaxed a while, and then went out for a walk. It was Sunday so we stayed around in camp.

We were back on parade again and went through all the same procedures. When the next weekend came, we were off. This time we decided to go to Nijmegen and check it out. We walked to the border, came to Well, had a few beers there, the barmaid smiling as usual and being friendly. We took the bus to Nijmegen.

We arrived at Nijmegen bus station just after 14.00 hrs. We took a slow walk up to the town. There were quite a number of bars jam-packed. We started out in a bar on Hertogstraat called *The Cosy Bar*. There was also another bar joined to it which belonged to the wife. The husband ran the *Cosy* bar sometimes with the help of the wife and the sons. There was always a barman in the wife's bar. We introduced ourselves and found that this family was a very friendly one. We went around and checked out many other bars and decided that the *Cosy* will be our usual bar.

Nijmegen was the town where it was all happening. Soldiers were coming from distant parts of Germany to spend the weekend in Nijmegen. On a Friday, Saturday and Sunday nights, the whole town was buzzing, even through the week on a Wednesday night. We came down if we were not prevented from doing so.

Nijmegen was also a place that was Roman from a long time ago. It was also the place of the biggest airborne operation in history, along with Arnhem and other places. The Germans had fuses already laid to blow the road bridge, but they were removed in the night by Jan van Hoof.

Nijmegen is the oldest town in the Netherlands. We often went in the parks for walks, and to get a good look at the surrounding areas. There was always a beautiful flower clock laid out below us as we looked down from the Belverdere Hotel.

With the weekend finished we got ourselves back safely to camp, and started preparing to go on exercise for two weeks. After this exercise, I ended up in the main hospital for ten days. Terry and Bill came often to see me. That same year, a girl in the camp came and ask me to accompany her to the flicks. I said to her, "You're that chap's girlfriend. I don't go out with other men's women."

She said, "We broke up, we're not in a relationship any more."

"Ok!" I said. "I'll escort you to the flicks and tomorrow I'll check out and see if what you told me was true."

"Do that," she said. "Everyone knows that I'm not in a relationship with Taffy any more."

"Wait a minute" I said. "You said 'Taff'! *which* 'Taff'? There were quite a lot of 'Taffys' running around in the camp – we even had one in our room."

"He's in the RAF (Royal Air Force)," she said, and came closer beside me.

"That one!" I said, "I know him well. The skinny one?"

"Yes," she said, "That's the one."

I escorted her to the flicks. The next day Taff bumped into me. He said, "So you're going out with Helen?"

"Wait!" I said. "It's not like that. She told me that she

was finished with you, and asked me to take her to the flicks."

I was glad when all that was behind me. Terry and Bill heard about it but paid no attention to it. The next weekend found us at the Well border. The girl behind the bar showed clearly that she liked me very much. We did not stay around long enough in Well for anything to happen. We took the bus to Nijmegen after we had a few bevvies.

*

It was the month of July in the second week when I was sitting in our usual cafe, and looking out onto the street, when I saw this tall, nice slim looking girl walking a child up and down the sidewalk. At first, I wanted to go straight out and say something to her. But when I saw the child, I changed my mind. I said to myself, she must be married, and I being the type who don't mess about with other men's women, I held myself back. I found out later, from the owner of the bar, that the girl lived next door and that the child belonged to her mother. I was really glad when I heard the news. I was now willing to make my move, the next time I should see her outside.

This same July we had a fete in our camp. Around 19.00 hrs some girls were sitting at a table next to ours. I was looking at this girl who was pouring whisky into a glass and knocking it back one after the other. I said to Terry and Bill, "Have you seen that girl with that whisky bottle? My God! She has *emptied* it!"

She was short and really good looking, and gave the impression that she was able to defend herself should the occasion arise. With the empty bottle, she waved us over.

We changed tables and sat at hers. Conversation started, and we found out that she was from Scotland. The other three were from places in Britain. The evening went on joyfully. None of us won the car that was the first prize, but we did enjoy the fete. At 22.00 hrs, the girls had to leave and return to the bus that was waiting there, and would take them back to their camp. I escorted the Scottish lass to the bus, gave her a kiss and got her address. When I got back to where Terry and Bill were, I found that most of the girls who were at other tables around, had left. I sat down at the table.

Terry said, "Well, are you going to see her again?"

I said, "Yes. She gave me her address and invited me up to Scotland."

"Aye, eh," Bill said. "Be careful of those jocks throwing their cabers about."

"I like the Scottish people," I said. "The only trouble is, I will not be able to understand all of what they say."

"Of course you'll understand them," Bill said. "They speak English as well."

Terry said, "It's only some of the old ones who get into the Scottish dialect, then you're *really* in trouble."

"I like the lass," I told them. "But I see that she likes her whisky. There's no doubt about that from what we saw today."

When the fete was ended, we joined up with some other soldiers from other regiments who were stationed at our camp. There were now about ten of us.

Later, I bought an old black Opel Capitan for 50 German marks. All the others thought I had lost a screw for doing so. It turned out that the car was very trustworthy. It took us to many places. And I had friends in the REME (Royal Electrical Mechanical Engineers) who made sure that the car was in good condition.

We took a new route to Nijmegen. We went through Weeze, Goch, Kranenburg and then down to the border. After many journeys the border guards got used to seeing us and the old car. One time, we actually took ten people in the car to Nijmegen. There was always room in the boot, but we did not do that very often.

We were in Nijmegen one weekend when a fair was taking place. I remembered that I was in the *Cosy* bar when the news came that the Dutch police had nicked one of our mates. I knew who it was, he was a good soldier. He never really got himself mixed up with anything to do with the police or the law. I was furious, throbbing and ready to burst like a ball that had been pumped with too much air. I got to the police building, went through some strange doors, and came to a desk with one of the officers sitting there. I approached the desk, raging mad, and said: *"Where is he? Where have you got him? Let him go now?"*

The police officer was trying to calm me down, but I swept all that was on the desk, with one quick movement, upon the ground. Suddenly, I saw another officer coming from my left side with our mate. I went over and said, "Are you ok, mate?" He said that he was by shaking his head, then the officers said that he could leave and that they had taken the wrong man. What a night that was! When we got back to camp we talked about nothing else but what had happened at the fair.

Our party increased so much that at the weekend we had about four to five cars making the trip to Nijmegen.

Sometimes too, we got a couple of Americans or Canadians cars that came along.

One day in camp I bumped into a chap from Dundee in Scotland. We played darts almost every night in the canteen. He invited me up to Dundee to see his family. I went and it was an interesting visit. The mother knew I had not known what haggis was like, so she cooked it specially for me that day. I hate to say this but when I got into it, I still don't know what it tasted like. I showed my respect and said that I had enjoyed it. The mother too, would not give anyone breakfast until I came out of bed and came down the stairs. Jock kept on reminding me of that.

*

It was good to be back at camp, and into the old routine again. It was also good to be back and getting down to Nijmegen. I don't know why, but when I turned 21 we all stayed in camp. We were all in the canteen. It was getting on and I had quite a lot down me already. I left and went to the wc. When I came back, the guys had a glass there for me, but I didn't know that there were all sorts of drinks in it. I sat down and started drinking. After about half an hour, I felt as if the devil had taken hold of me. I started sweeping all that was on the table, with my hands, onto the floor.

Chairs and tables were flying everywhere. The barmaid must have called the Military police. I was standing on a table, staggering like a pole in a storm when I saw this dog handler came in with one of their dogs. I think it was an Alsatian. I jumped down from the table, ran over to where the dog was, and sunk my teeth into its neck. The police handler was trying to get me off the dog; my friends, too, were there and tugging me away. The dog ran away, and out the door which was left half open. The handler went after it. Then I remembered nothing more.

I was supposed to be in charge of setting up some tents on the Monday morning. When I woke up, there was no one in the room. All the beds were neatly made. My head was thumping like mad, those men with their hammers, hammering away. I managed to get myself to the wash basins, cleaned up a bit, dressed into working gear, and then made my way up to the working compound. Every one around knew that it had been my 21st birthday the night before. The commanding Officer saw me and said, "How's your head, Granville?"

I said, "Not too bad, sir!" I thought that I would have been in trouble for being late, and failing to be there for the setting up of the tents. I thanked God that everything turned out just as I had expected it to. Terry and Bill could not get me to wake up, so they had left me alone to sleep it off.

That week I got letters from the girl in Scotland. She asked me to come up. She lived just outside Edinburgh. I went. It was cold and snowy. The snow was knee deep. I met her parents, and the old man asked me something in the old Scots language. I hadn't a clue of what he said. The girl had to translate for me. I took her to the flicks in Edinburgh and to a restaurant. Back at her place, in my room, there was a big grandfather clock over my bed. It chimed a quarter to the hour; on the hour; a quarter past the hour; and half past the hour. Next morning I was asked how I slept. I told them not too good because of the chiming of the clock, not to mention the ticking of it, with the long pendulum beneath swinging left to right and back. I did enjoy my stay in Scotland.

When I got back to camp, I told terry and Bill and some other lads about my trip. A couple of weeks later, Terry, Bill and I were off to Nottingham. Terry was going to get married, and we started teasing, telling him about the end of his freedom days. He didn't pay much attention to what we said. I saw Jane, and we had a chat. She had a new boyfriend and was expecting his child.

*

The wedding of Terry and Trisha was great. Trisha in her white gown, with a long train behind her along with two bridesmaids. Terry in his tight grey suit, the teddy boy type, and again there was the tie that was as thin as a shoestring. The reception went down well and we all had a good time. Bill and I came back to camp a week before Terry did. We got back and started preparing for the big exercise – 6 weeks away from camp.

All these exercises were good. They kept us busy, learning all the things to do if ever there was a war. They kept us in shape as well.

We arrived back from the six weeks exercise all stinky and mucky, yet we had lots of changes of working clothes to put on. Well, it was the weather you know. And what can you do about that? – nothing. That weekend we headed straight for Nijmegen.

A lot had taken place down there as well. Something great happened to me. The girl I had seen walking her mother's child along the footpath, came out her door that was a couple of doors away from the *Cosy*. She crossed the street and went to the automatic where you can get all sorts of things to eat. As she crossed back and came to her door, I was there. I called her by her name for the owner of the *Cosy* had told it to me. She was shocked. "Who are you?" she asked. "What do you want?"

I came straight to the point. "I would like to go out with you."

"I can't," she said. "My parents wouldn't allow it."

Then I heard someone calling her name from above the stairs. She said, "Coming," told me she had to go and that she'll see me another time. She left me at the bottom of the stairs, closed the door and went up to her parents. When I got back inside the *Cosy*, everyone wanted to know how it went. I told them.

*

Six of us finally made it to Amsterdam. We drove up from Nijmegen. The distance is about 128 kilometres. When we got there, we parked up in a road beside a canal. One of the chaps said, "That's clever, you'll be able to find where you park the car, next to the water."

"What are you talking about?" I asked. "Almost every street has a canal beside it, with bridges crossing over."

We went straight away and started looking around.

Amsterdam was a small fishing village long ago, around the 13th century. Now it's one of Europe's main cities. We found a bar and stayed there for a while. Then one after the other we visited the other bars. We came along the street where women sit in windows – the *red light district*. While we were in a bar, one of the chaps said that he saw a nice one in the window. We said to him, "Don't tell us, go and test it out."

He said, "Maybe." After we had visited quite a few bars, and it was really getting late, we decided to go and see if we could locate the car. It wasn't that easy. We just couldn't find the street where the car had been parked. All the streets looked the same with bridges everywhere. It was now early morning, and still we saw no sign of the black Opel Capitan. In order for all of us not to get into trouble back at camp, some of the chaps took trains back, while Terry, Bill and I kept on searching for the car. After a few hours, we spotted it – exactly where we had left it. I opened the door, set the key in the starter, gave it a turn, then I heard the car engine as it came to life. We drove back to camp, got back late, and had lots of explaining to do. There were no charges given out, and everthing was back to normal.

Summer camp found us at Garmisch Partenkirchen, next to the Zugspitze, the highest peak in Germany. It's about 2962 metres high. We drove about 760 kilometres to get to Garmisch. The area is beautiful, snow-covered mountain; the houses with trays of flowers decorating the balconies; and the cows with bells hanging around their necks.

Summer camp is always great. This one was special. We really enjoyed ourselves even with some strenuous things thrown in. There came a day when I had to drive some soldiers a fair way up the mountain. They were going to climb the rest of the mountain to the top. Helicopters were flying all the time overhead. Terry and Bill stayed back at base camp helping the cook and peeling spuds.

I drove quite slowly up the mountain, along the small winding path. The drop below was very deep, and I had no intention of going down there. I reached the destination where the truck could not go any further. On the return journey, I drove the truck down a very steep gradient. The three other soldiers who came with me for company, got out and started walking. They saw how dangerous it was. In front of me was a track, and then the dangerous deep. The truck moved slowly down, I had to turn left on the track. There were no barriers to stop you from going over into the deep. I turned the wheel so that the truck could hug the dirt cliff on the left. It was important that I didn't make any mistake at this point, the truck and I would have fallen over the right side. Luckily, everything went well, and the other soldiers, along the track, climbed again back on board. We made it safely back to base camp. I told Terry and Bill about the dangerous mountain, and how scary it was.

*

On a day when we were free to do whatever we wanted to, we found ourselves sitting outside one of the bars, and drinking from a glass boot. After that we went to Garmisch swimming pool. There were two pools, one for the grown ups, and a small one for the young kids. Typical for us soldiers, we wound up playing in the kiddies pool. The sun was hot, it was a nice day, and we enjoyed ourselves.

Then a day came when most of us had to walk over mountains for 30 kilometres. Now I must say, I was really shattered, but all in all the summer camp went down well.

*

We got back to camp and heard the sad news of one of the Canadians who had died in car crash on the Nijmegen/ Arnhem roundabout. We stayed there for some time, then we went to our usual cafe. The barman gave us more info. The Canadian had come down, met his girlfriend, they came to the cafe, stayed a while, then it was time for him to drive back to camp when the accident happened. We heard some time later that his parents had come over from Canada to Nijmegen, and visited the place where the accident took place, and to speak personally with those who knew their son.

Weeks after that I had a date with Wilhelmina, the girl who I had seen walking her mother's child along the side walk. Terry said to me one day, "Now you're going out with the Queen of the Netherlands."

"She's not queen anymore," I told him, "Juliana is queen."

"I only said that because your girl has the same name as the old queen," Terry explained sipping at his beer.

Bill asked, "Have you met the parents yet?"

"Give it time for God's sake!" I replied. "Let me settle in and find my way. I think though that her dad would be hard to get around."

Terry said, "Bribe him, take him out, get him drunk, then tell him any old thing."

"No. I can't do that," I said. "I have to be honest with the parents. What they see is what they get."

"The Dutch are friendly, so you should have no problem there," Bill stated. "And this town is very friendly. There's hardly ever any trouble around. See the little kids, walking all on their own, even in the dark of night; and getting home safely. If it was in any other country, they would have been kidnapped, raped and murdered."

"You're right," I agreed with him. "The place has always been friendly, but I don't know if it was so when the Romans were here."

Terry said those Romans were wild and murderous. One thing I must say, they kept good government. They always took on other people's customs whenever they capture them. They were hard fighting men, never afraid to die."

Bill said, "Their women were almost the same, ready at any time to take the dagger as soon as things went wrong."

Terry said, looking straight at me, "If your girl is anything like the old queen of the Netherlands, then you have found yourself a good catch. But... I mean, your girl is not in charge of a country or ever will be."

"How do you know that?" I asked him.

"Because it's not possible. Some things are possible but not this one." Terry explained. "Wilhelmina had a very strong love for her people, they came first, no matter what. She was a woman who loved human beings. She was very brave and courageous."

"You've started now," I told Terry, "so you'd better let us have the rest."

"Ok! Wilhelmina was the daughter of King William 3rd. Her mother was Emma of Waldeck-Pyrmont. When her father died, she took over the thrown while her mother was in charge. Wilhelmina married Duke Henry of Mecklenburg-Schwerin; and later was pregnant with Juliana. During World War I, she kept the Netherlands in a neutral position."

"Well done Terry," I said, "you know quite a lot about the Dutch monarchy. I too, am interested in royals, but never got really attracted to the Dutch monarchy. I know bits and pieces, of course. I think Wilhelmina sticks out a lot because of her personality, and knew what her duty was. Now, I know a lot about the British monarchy. Some old stories state that Brutus from Troy was the first king. But I start off with King Alfred the Great. Before he became king he fought side by side with his brother Aethelred. Alfred was only 17 years old at that time. He took over from his brother but he had no intention of becoming king. It was through him that England became so great. He fought off the Danish invasion and made peace with them. I will tell you, even up to now, it is the English people who run the country. It's *they* who really decide who'll be Prime Minister, or double Prime Ministers. The English people love their kings, queens, princes and princesses, and all the royal house."

"In that you're right," said Bill. "I've read a bit of English history and most of what you said is correct. Take for instance when Richard I was on the throne. The English people loved Richard and paid a great ransom to get him back in one piece."

"We all seem to know quite a bit about some history," I said. "Anyway, I'm now going to tell you of something that happened to me one weekend when both of you were on duty, and could not make it to Nijmegen.

I was at the *Cosy*, standing in the doorway, just taking it easy when this drunk came right up to me, and for no reason wahtsoever, he began to push me. I said to him, *Go away, leave me alone.* He went away a few times but came back and kept on pushing me. The last time he came back and did that, I gave him a right and flattened him there and then. When I looked up at the flat on my left, there was a window half open, and a woman with a pot of flowers in her hand ready to throw down on my head. The woman was Wilhelmina's mother. Their flat was two doors away from the *Cosy*.

"See, we can't leave you alone before you're getting yourself into trouble," Terry told me.

"I did keep myself out of trouble. But that guy was really asking for it." I answered Terry.

We found another bar that we liked and visited it often. Next to this bar was a dancing place. We went there a few times. I remembered once that Horace got himself a girlfriend from Nijmegen. She lived not very far from the main station. Horace happened to be on duty one weekend, and he could not make it to Nijmegen. The rest of us went down. It was around 21.30 pm when we visited the dance place. We entered the door with the bar on the left-hand side. There at the bar, on a stool, was Horace's girl with a bloke's arms around her. I went over and said to the bloke, "She's already taken, *beat it!*" I was already half drunk from the other cafe, and to tell you the truth I don't know what happened after I had spoken to the chap.

Next morning I woke up on the dance floor with lots of broken glasses around. I managed to get myself up, still with my head pounding like when they're laying foundations for a building. I felt a bit shaky as well. I stood up avoiding being cut by broken glass that was there all around. I started examining myself to see if I was cut or bruised. I was ok. No damage to myself. I heard later from the cleaners the story they had heard from the barman.

Apparently, the bloke who had his arms around Horace's girl, was a blackbelt judo expert. When I heard that I said to myself, "I was really drunk, yes I was." I also lost my passport. The guys who were with me knew nothing about what had happened. I had left them at the cafe just around the corner, and had gone alone to the dance place. When they came looking for me, the place had already been shut up with me sprawled across the dance floor like scrambled eggs. It was Sunday morning when the cleaners came and my mates had the chance of getting in.

It was coming up to 12pm on Sunday when we were walking along to go up to our usual cafe. I spotted the same chap who had been n the dance place, and who had his hands around Horace's girlfriend, leaning on his polished car. I went up to him and said, "I'm not drunk now. Would you like to try on me what you did to me in the dance place last night when I was drunk?"

He said nothing. My mates came and took me away, saying, "Leave it. Forget about it. It's over and done with." We left him there leaning on his car, and we went up to the *Cosy*.

Things started to go well with Wilhelmina and myself. The father was still a bit hard. He had grounded her for six months because she came in late. And another time she had to be in by 9pm. I would pass along and she would throw bits of paper down with writings on them. After that things became much easier, and I was allowed to visit their home.

The mates and I found another cafe on the same street as the *Cosy*; but at the other end. We went and checked it out. There were many Anericans and Canadians and Germans inside. Every time we went in, we were welcomed, and of course, the Americans had a name for us. It was *"Limey."* We also found another cafe just below Kronenburg park. So we had four favourite bars to visit. Of course, we visited other places, but didn't stay long. There was a nice cafe just by the church but it was too packed. It was shaped like a horse shoe. It was a downstairs cellar cafe. We realized that if fire broke out, it would have been very dangerous to free ourselves from that crowd, so we scrubbed it from our list.

One night, we were at the bar down by Kronenburg park. There were many people in the bar. The Dutch had this game of playing dice, and the loser has to buy every one in the bar drinks. The beer glasses were very small and I found when it was nearing midnight, I had drunk so many of these glasses of beer, that I became awfully drunk, then found myself being sober again. It is a very strange experience, and this was the first time that such a thing happened to me.

The next night we were there again. There was a girl there all on her own, I went and chatted with her, and got one of the chaps to date her. He later married her and had children. The carnival came around again, and we enjoyed ourselves, still acting like kids. After the weekend had finished, we all went back to camp, and were ready to go on our yearly six weeks exercise.

*

The exercise was a tough one. They made us think that a war was on. If we got captured, we were held in some old farmhouse, our boots taken away from us, and then they started interrogating us. They wanted to know all our details. Some of us gave them a hard time.

There was one time when it was really cold, I just couldn't feel my toes at all, and we had nothing to eat, because we had to walk so many kilometres where we would then be fed. That night, in my sleeping bag, I cursed the army, I was angry with myself for being in this situation. I tossed and I turned all night through but sleep just wouldn't come. Then morning came and as we were walking down a track, we saw one of the enemy landrovers coming towards us. At the side of the track, there was a deep gutter, and without thinking, we all threw ourselves into the gutter. I remember it clearly now for there were some dry sticks that were there pointing upwards, and one of them just missed by left eye. Was I lucky or what?

We arrived at the next point just in time for breakfast, and then we were off again.

I must really say that the exercise really taught us something. And we all thought back to those soldiers who actually had to go to war. We were fit and ready. If there was a war, we knew what we had to do. But there was no war, and we were only peacetime soldiers being trained just in case there was one.

One weekend, after midnight on Sunday, we were travelling back to our camp. Just after we had passed through the Dutch border, and into Germany, we noticed a car that was behind us, and not wanting to pass us. I told the guys that there was something wrong. I slowed down, and the car behind me slowed down as well. I brought my car to a standstill, and the one behind did the same. I got out and went back to the driver's side, while a couple of

Germans got out from the back seat. I said to the driver: "What the hell are you doing following me like that? Is there something wrong?"

Terry, Bill and another was there beside me. The lights of both car were shining onto the road.

"*You,*" One of the chaps who came out from the back, said, "*you* are the one who's being going out with the girlfriend of Hans!"

Terry came in and said, "You've definitely got the wrong bloke. Jarvis has never messed around with other men's women. That I can assure you he doesn't do."

Bill said, "Where is your proof? Come on, get going and leave us be."

I said, " I know what it is. Back in the village near to the camp. I was in a bar and playing this flipper machine. I saw this blonde girl who came a few times and looked at me. I left that machine and went to the back to play on another one. She came there too, so I left the bar."

"Ohzo," said the driver, and revved up his car. Those who came out of the back went back in and they drove off leaving us there still talking about it.

Not far back was the Dutch border, and the lights of Nijmegen could still be seen. We all got back into the Opel Capitan, and we continued our journey to camp.

Not long after, my marriage came about, that of Bill as well. Then all three of us were posted to Singapore.

4

Marriage & postings to Singapore

It was October month and Wilhelmina's family were very busy organizing the marriage. I was not myself at all. I managed to stay out of trouble, still fit and healthy. The aunt of Wilhelmina was a very great help. It was at the place where I stayed the night before the wedding.

Wilhelmina wore a long white gown with a long train. Her sister acted as bridesmaid. I was in my army best with six guards of honour. The whole main street was packed with people, and it was hard for traffic to pass by. They hadn't seen a wedding like that in years. There were three guards of honour on one side of the steps and another three on the opposite side. We came to the town hall which was an old Roman building, and we went in and the ceremony started. I was absolutely glad when it was all over. You know I wanted to be married, and so did Wilhelmina, but when the actual day came, I think I was somewhere in the sky. I relaxed, and felt much better when we got to the reception. It was in a building half of which belongs to the British legion and the other half was a restaurant.

When I was back in Nottingham in the earlier years, my drink was milkshake. Now I was drinking beer. At the reception, I didn't drink so much but I enjoyed the whole evening. We stayed around longer than we were supposed to, chatting with the guests. When we finally got back to Wilhelmina's parents' place, we stood outside and could not get into the door. From stories I heard from what the Dutch families do when there was a wedding, I was expecting something, but nothing like this. We stood for at least half an hour before someone turned up with the keys to the door.

When Wilhelmina and I were dating, we did more kissing than anything else. We just took this easy. Now on this our wedding night, alone with no one to disturb us, we did what most newly married people would do – knowing each other intimately.

The next day was strange. I woke up and it hit me: *I'm a married man*. My God! Do you know what that means? I'm not free any more to do whatever I like before first consulting my wife. So that's what married life is all about? Well, I enjoyed it.

*

We moved to Germany to a place that was very religious, candles burning in the shop windows everywhere, with a small old tower in the middle of the square. The flat we had was long and small with the walls crumbling in when touched. I tried many times to fill in the gaps that were in the wall, but that too was a failure.

Wilhelmina got pregnant and there was something wrong so I went to the German doctor there in the place where we lived, and he ordered that she be taken into the hospital. Later, all went well, except that we had a quarrel, and she went back to her parents.

We sorted it all out and later moved to the village that was near to the camp. There was a nice flat there and we took it over. The German family lived below with two children. We became very friendly with that family. For even when we moved and went into a big house in the same village, we visited the German family often. I was on duty when Wilhelmina was taken to the main hospital for pregnancy. I went up the following day. She had a girl and was very pleased.

Wilhelmina became pregnant again, and again, I was on guard duty and had to go up to the main hospital the next day. She had a girl, but had to be helped by the doctors to bring it out safely.

In June the next year, we were posted to Singapore, but we went to England where we would catch the plane. Before that we went down to Nottingham to the wedding of Bill and Susan.

On the day of the wedding, Susan wore a beautiful embroidered long white gown. She had two bridesmaids beside her. Bill had on a suit just like Terry had when he got married. And again, there was that thin tie like a shoestring. There were many people present and the reception was splendid.

End of June saw us all on the plane. Terry and Trisha, Bill and Susan, Wilhelmina, the two kids and myself. We were flying off to Singapore.

*

Singapore was known around the 3rd century as the *"island at the end of the peninsular."* The Chinese called it *"Sea town."* Later it became the *"Lion City."*

First settlers came 1298-1299. Around the 14th century it was ruled by five kings of Ancient Singapura. The British were looking for a place for their fleet to stop any attack by the Dutch,

Singapore turned out to be just that place.

Singapore was founded in 1819 by Sir Thomas Stamford Raffles. In 1826 Singapore, Malacca, and Penang falls under the British rule. Raffles landed on Singapore 29th January 1819 and established it as a trading station.

Singapore was attacked during the second World War on 8th December 1941 at 4 am. The attackers came from the north. The Allied forces gave over to he Japanese on the 15th February 1942. The biggest surrender of British forces in history. The Japanese had power over Singapore from 1942-1945. In 1945 they surrendered. In April 1946 Singapore became a British Crown Colony.

*

What a beautiful island Singapore is, and with so many different races of people as well.

The plane came over a little runway – well it looked little from up there where we were. I said to Terry, "We're not going to make it. The runway is too small."

He said: "It looks so but the plane will land ok. It did and we all got off, took our transport to the place where we would stay. The clothes I had on were sticking to me and I wanted to get cleaned up and put on a new set of clothing.

The second child that we had was very young, it was only four months old, and it had its own passport, which wasn't really allowed, but this was a special case.

The place we stayed at was owned by a chinese family. It was very clean and tidy, and the family was very friendly.

That evening when Wilhelmina went to the shower, there were all these geckos upon the wall. She had never seen these things before, and was frightened of them. She started stamping saying,

"I want to go back home. Get me out of here!"

I said to her, "Calm yourself down, these things you see are not dangerous, they are house friendly. Just go and have your shower and you'll be ok."

She calmed down a bit, went and had her shower, came back and was still not totally pleased. But one thing that she noticed was that the place was so clean, that it was possible to eat off the floor.

We made it through that first night in the hotel, and for another couple of weeks while I was busy trying to find a good cheap house. I found a nice three bed room house on one of the roads going to our workplace. It had a big front garden with some big trees at the back. You had to make sure that the house windows and doors were safe with shutters against thieves.

Terry and Bill had also found nice homes and we all invited each other for house warming. It all went down well. Then we reported to our work place and started getting used to the lay out of the place.

There are a few things in Singapore that one has to be aware of. They are scorpions, pythons, malaria from mosquitos at night, spiders, geckos, houseflies, cockroaches, lizards. The largest snake in the world is the reticulated python. Apart from all that, it was not bad at all.

A few months we got to know Singapore much better. We located all the places that we should go for attraction and entertainment. Terry, Bill and I were in the same troop, and we did almost everything together. We had local who were also soldiers, but they didn't get the same pay as us who were from England. Working together went down well. There were no problems at all. Sometimes some of the locals would invite us to their houses.

I remember once, this Malaysian soldier, invited Wilhelmina and myself to his house and his family. Well actually, he and myself and a couple others were in a band. We played for the Prime Minister of Singapore and his political party. There was no opposition party in Singapore.

So, while Wilhelmina and I were walking up this dirt track with bins outside full of rubbish, a big massive fly came from one of the bins and came at us like a plane diving to bomb its target. But there were many more. We escape them. It was big and black – look more like a bee.

A few of the houses were on stilts and leaning so badly that I thought they would fall down. The malasian soldier (normally dressed in British uniform just like the rest of us), came to the front and greeted us. We went up some shaky steps and into the house. The house was like a palace with big thick carpets, and I never saw such a big fridge in all my life. This one reached up to the ceiling.

We sat down at the table in the dining place, which was the next room to the sitting room. When the meal was ready, his wife and kids sat around the table, and he sat on top of the table. He used his fingers to eat with, but he laid out knifes, spoons and forks or us. We enjoyed the meal and told him so.

We went to sit in the sitting room, and he brought a tray with something that look like jelly, wobbling, and with something over them that look like grated something. I later found out that it was grated coconut or something like that.

I wasn't planning at all of taking one of those things until he said to me, "Jarvis, try one."

I said to myself, "Oh my God, here we go."

I didn't want to offend them so I took one of those jelly things, and it found its way into my mouth. Looking at him with a pleasant face, I happen to bite the jelly, and at the same time, a liquid oozed out into my throat. It was horrible, but I sat there, and slowly, I let the whole thing down my throat without offending the family. Later, we thank them for a pleasant evening and we went back home.

Our stay in Singapore was working out well. I did a lot of sports such as athletics, football and cricket. I remembered that we went from Singapore up to Penang, and there, we had a cricket match with the Australian cricket team. They were on tour. You won't believe this but I actually faced the two fast bowlers Australia had at that time. To tell you the truth, I was hit more times than I hit the ball. They put us in three times and still we could not make the score which they had made in one innings. It was great fun.

We had a few jungle exercises that opened up our eyes when we think back of those veterans who had to defend Singapore. While the British had been looking out to sea thinking that the Japanese would come that way, they the Japanese actually came through that thick jungle. And I was in there experiencing it myself. We've been through some hard exercises, but war is even harder.

Later on, when things were more relaxed and we had holidays, a number of us married couples along with children, went to a far away island that was near to the place where they had filmed *South Pacific*. Before we went over to the island, we stayed at a hotel on the mainland. One night, we had to move out and go to one of the outdoor houses because the King of Sarawak was coming there to stay.

We had mosquito nets around all the beds. The next morning, I was covered in bumps all over my body.

We hired a small boat from the village nearby, and the man took all of us over to the island. It was small, with clear water. One could see the white sand at the bottom with all the different coloured fishes swimming around.

Terry said to Trisha: "You're not going to find this back in Nottingham."

She answered, "You're right, it's a beautiful little island."

Just in front of us, not far away, was another little island. Bill said, "See who gets to it first." We all rushed into the clear warm water, and started swimming as if we were in some race. Then we stopped. I said, "It looks near, but it is some distance from us." We all turned around and went back and relaxed on the burning white sand.

There were a few coconut trees on the island. There was one hanging over the sea, as if it was going to fall into it. It was laden with green coconuts. I said to the others, "Do you want some nice fresh water." I went over to another coconut tree and started to climb it. I got right to the top, and made my way into the middle of it, then I started yanking the nuts off and down onto the white sand. We all enjoyed the fresh coconut water.

Susan got brown quickly but it wasn't as bad as the Scottish man who was as white as a sheet, and had never been in the sun before this time. At the end of the day, he looked terrible. Still, we all enjoyed the day and was taken back by the man in the boat back to the mainland.

Our stay in Singapore was coming to an end. This island is really beautiful, and if ever I get the chance, I definitely would go back.

The disbandment came around very quickly and we handed over to the Singapore army. After all the celebrations, the day came when we were to leave Singapore behind us, and head back to England.

From there our flight would take us back to Germany.

Our stay in Singapore was great. It had now come to an end and it was time to return to England and then to Germany.

5

High jinx in Germany

After all the celebrations we prepared ourselves for the trip back to England. We would stay a few days around, then be on our way to Germany.

We arrived in Germany and Terry and Trisha, Bill and Susan got themselves quarters and moved in straight away. I took Wilhelmina down to Nijmegen where she stayed with her parents. I stayed in my new camp for a few months, then I got a nice big flat in a German village.

The block I was staying in had a direct look onto the big main square. Inside my room were three other soldiers. I learn later, that this regiment were out in the field for about 9 months in the year. That was heavy. They did a lot of exercises. I did enjoy my first exercise which lasted for two weeks. I was now in the mood to tackle the rest.

One night I was in my block just coming up to midnight. I happen to look out the window and onto the square. I couldn't believe my eyes of what I was seeing. I thought at first, I was seeing monkeys crawling about the square. I call some of the blokes in the room to witness what I was seeing. They said, "Oh! it's just those guys in the block below us. We often see that when they are drunk or high."

"High?" I inquired.

"You know, high on smoke. They take this stuff, and it makes them do foolish things."

I said, "Ok! I understand. But I didn't really know how one would feel when they had that stuff inside of them.

A couple of days later, I found myself visiting that same block, and became friends with a few soldiers there. It was a block with mainly coloured soldiers either from Africa, the Seychelles, or from the West Indies. We started listening to Calypsos, and this brought back some memories from when I was back home and listening to Lord Kitchener or to the Sparrow. These were great Calypso singers. The trouble is, I was accustomed to those nice songs of the 60's.

I was inside a room belong to a chap from England. He was really crazy about Uriah Heep, Deep Purple and Led Zeppelin. I remember one time he played an LP of Led Zeppelin and one side was just about one song. I must admit, at the time I wasn't into those songs. But later on, as I visited more, I got to understand what the groups were playing, and I was able to pierce through the noise, and get to understand the lyrics – the words.

A very strange experience happened to me one night I visited the block below me. This chap gave me a cigarette, he said it is cool, it will make you feel good. I took a couple puffs of the cigarette. Then later on when I went back to my room, I was laying on my bed, on my right side. Suddenly, I felt my left leg rising up to the ceiling. I stayed there for a while because I wanted to see what would happen. I jumped up and grabbed my leg, and it was there, still on the bed, and not rising up. From that time onwards, I said to myself, that I would keep away from all that stuff. I don't want anything to do with it.

A few months later, we formed a group. First, there was an officer, but later, he withdrew. Then a German came with his own equipment He was a real professional but he still stayed with us for a while. We got a few gigs. I remember one time we went to the camp of the Royal Scots guards. We were told if they don't like you, they would start flinging things at you. When we played for them, they actually enjoyed it. The night went down well.

Now and then, Terry and Bill would come into the camp at night and we would go to the Naaifi and play some games.

One night in my block, I was woken up late at night from a commotion out in the corridor. I got up, opened the door and saw a few chaps there. There was this well-built chap, young, only in his under pants, and having a bayonet in his right hand and threatening the rest. I knew him very well. I went out and approached him, asking him to give the bayonet over. All the other chaps were surprised when he handed over the bayonet. Then everything was quiet and peaceful again.

The following week a group of us were walking in the town which wasn't far from our camp. There were a few German police cars patrolling. We went through a shopping arcade and was met by a group of young tough Germans. One of them, a blonde one, blurted out,"Go back home to England."

I went to the front. I looked him staright in the face, "We're going to stay here as long as it's possible and you can't do anything about it. Get out of our way, and let us pass. We're not here to make trouble with the likes of you. We're here to protect your country, don't you know that?"

Someone in our group shouted, *"SOUR KRAUT!"* and spat on the tile. The small German group moved closer to us. We were ready to get into a fray should it come to that. Unfortunately, some German police came through the arcade, as if they were expecting some trouble, and so we dispersed without anything happening.

*

A great big exercise came about, and we all left camp, and went a long way into Germany. There were tanks all over the place and we moved very often. As soon as we got into one place, the order came for us to move. So as soon as we had settled in, we had to break camp, and be off. It was hard going, we learned a lot from it.

When I got back to camp I went around looking for a house where Wilhelmina and the kids and I could live in. Terry and Bill drove me around. We came in a small village and found some brand new flats. I was lucky, there was only one left on the third floor, so I quickly grabbed it. The next building on the right was a German pub, so we went in there and had a drink. I let them know who I was, and that I'd be living next door. A big man who was sitting there in the corner came to the bar, he looked at me and said: "You from Africa?"

I said, "No. England,"

He said, "Nein, Africa?"

I said, "Nein. England."

He said, " Your parents? Africa?"

I said, "Nein, England."

He had this worried look upon his face, that told me he was baffled. He finally said, "You, Schnapps?"

To tell you the truth, I didn't know what Schnapps was. The woman behind the bar was middle-aged; she took from the shelf, a bottle with some white stuff in it. Then she got some glasses, which were very small, and poured the white stuff from the bottle into the glasses. Every one of us in the bar took the glasses. I saw them all flung the glasses to their mouth and down into their throats. I was there still sipping at mine. The man beside me, showed me how to drink it properly. I did. Then I asked for a beer quickly, and drank it as fast as I could. Every one was grinning. They all found it funny. Even Terry and Bill. It was a nice 45 minutes we spent in that pub getting to know my neighbours.

Our music group was doing well. We got a place where we could play every Saturday night. Inside our own camp there was going to be a big dance and they wanted a group to play for them. We had no drummer or bass guitarist yet we beat three other groups who had drummers and bass guitarists. The night of the dance went down well, and everyone enjoyed the music.

*

I had to now go down to Nijmegen and fetch Wilhelmina and the kids. The flat was now ready. When Wilhelmina arrived, she liked the place, and was in a good mood.

The kids got themselves into their schools and were pleased. I got to know a little more about the village and its inhabitants. I found out that there was another pub in the village, It opened on a Wednesday night. The one next to me would shut up and every one would trail up to the top one. There was also a bus service that came regularly to take people to the town.

I myself was now deep into athletics,and I had to keep myself really superfit. Sometimes when I'm training in the village, the kids would come with me. It wa a long run, and I could see on their faces, when we first started that they didn't like it. Later on, they got used to it. I found myself doing the 100 metres, the 200 metres, 400 metres, the high jump and the shot put. Then at the end of the meeting, I had to go into the 4 by 100 metres relay. I do not know how I did it all, but it all happened.

I remember once I was at the German stadium in the town practicing the shot put. A woman came up to me and told me I was doing it wrong. She showed me how it was done. I took her advice, and it worked well in the next athletic meeting we had. This woman turned out to be the sister of the captain of our athletics team, and she was Champion in the women's shot put. Some officials from the stadium approached me concerning taking part in certain events. I would have taken up the challenge but it wasn't that easy to do so.

In the village where I lived, they had a football team, they asked me to come and have a game. I went and played in goal. When the game was over they asked me if I could play regularly, but that wasn't at all possible due to army regulations and other commitments.

I was now strong and unbeatable in the 100 metres race. This thing was on my shoulder, every one was trying to thrash me. I had to keep myself really fit, and I also had to be careful because I felt like a super power. There was one meeting though, where I was all favourite to win the shot put. Something strange happened when my turn came to throw. For some unknown reason, the shot acted strange, or it felt strange between my fingers, and when I threw it, it didn't go very far. I had three goes and they were all a mess. Everyone in the stadium was shocked when they saw my performance.

At this time Terry and Bill were getting ready to finish their term. We were in the Naafi playing snooker just around lunch time.

Terry said to me, "When your time come to leave, what are you going to do? Go back to Nottingham or stay in Nijmegen?

I said to him, "I've already started making plans to try and get work in Nijmegen, and also a place to stay. What about you?"

Terry said, "I"ll try to get a job as a bus driver, you can't go wrong there."

"And you Bill? I asked. "Are you planning to go back to the yard?"

"I don't think so," he said. " I probably do the same as Terry. Or try to get a job with some technical firm."

"We've had some good times together, haven't we? And we did pretty good seeing how young we were." I said.

Terry came around where I was and whispered in my ear.

" I burst out with joy and said, "That really is great news." He had told me that Trisha was pregnant.

I said to him, "That's where it all start, my friend. Getting up all hours of the night, with changing nappies, and making the feed. You had better prepare yourself."

"Piece of cake," he answered back.

"And what about Susan?" I asked bill. "Nothing yet?

Come on what are you doing?"

Bill said, "We've tried ever so hard, but nothing."

Terry said, "Maybe later on you'll have them all coming without stopping."

Bill said, "Oh, no. We only want two – a boy and a girl."

"What if you get two boys or two girls?"

"That will do us fine," Bill said.

We finished the snooker game and then went back to work.

I hate it when I am at an athletic meeting, and at the end of the day, there are only about a couple of points between the two top teams. I was never really good at maths, but the Captain and other members were already busy working out what position we had to come in to win the competition. The last race of the day was the four by 100 metres relay. So many things could happen in this race, that I just didn't let them get to me. I remember once in training, the runner came in while I was just outside the box waiting. As he got to a certain mark which I had placed there, I began running. Now I had to be careful that I didn't run away too fast and left him stranded, still with the batten. And I had to make sure he came into the box at the right time. Then I would wip my hand back, and should feel the batten in it, hold on to it, and speed away. But these things didn't happen like that. The runner had come in too fast and overan me, what a muddle that was. But later we got it right.

At the meeting I was in lane three. Instructions were coming to me left right and center, telling me who to watch out for, and what I have to do when I hit the bend. Make sure the batten change is good, keep it in the box. My head was really filled up with instructions. But they were good instuctions.

There was a lot of pressure knowing that I was the last leg runner, and it all depends on me to deliver. The stadium was packed on this last day of the meeting. All the high officials and officers were present. Wilhelmina and the kids were there too. Terry, Trisha, Bill and Susan were all there too.

I made a mark on the track as a sign for me when the runner comes in, and hits that mark, then I will run off, and get in to the box, hoping that when I'm half way in the box, I'll receive the batten. I knew the chap who was starting was very good, he was fast, and disciplined, he was like me, wanting everything to go down well.

Then I heard the starter saying, *"On your marks! set!"* then the gun went off. Watching, from where I was, the runners starting off, was something I would always remember. I kept my eyes on our starter, he did pretty well, passed the batten beautifully within the box to the other runner. Still keeping my eyes on the race, I saw that someone had dropped the batten, but it wasn't our runner, he was still going. I now know my time was coming up to take over. I waited on my mark, and when the runner came in and hit the mark I had made, I ran off like hell, and when I got in the box, my right hand went back, and the runner slapped the batten into it. There was no stopping me now. I was off like a bullet. Coming up to the end I saw out the corner of my eye that this runner was neck and neck with me. I heard the great shouting coming from the stadium, from the spectators. I already knew what I was going to do to get rid of that other runner, and win the race. I saw the tape just in front of me, and I made a leap as if I wanted to fly. I hit the tape first and went crashing into the cinders on the track and grated my right knee. We had won the meeting and everyone in our team were celebrating.

*

Bill's birthday party came around and we all enjoyed ourselves. I remember, Bill was telling some of the other guests about how we met in the train yard at Nottingham. They found it rather interesting. After Bill's birthday party, we all left camp and went out for three days exercise.

This exercise turned out to be a very strange and weird one. For a start there was this officer, and I just didn't like him, but I still had respect for him because he was an officer. The men I worked with knew that as well. I think he was trying to give me a hard time. But I did something that showed him that I was no fool, and that I was a good soldier and knew what I was doing. I had an attachment of 20 soldiers, and every one of us got on as if we were from the same family. No matter what rank you were, things went down well, and we all worked well together.

Leaving camp, one of the trailers broke down. We just had to get another. We hit the autobahn and was on our way. On the left-hand side, after about an hours drive, we saw a drive in with men working there. We carried on and turned off later into a big forest area. I told the chaps that I had a strange feeling about this place. We got in and started camouflaging ourselves like we normally did whenever we went out on exercise. Our three ton truck was like a little house, comfortable, and yet it had lots of drums in it. When evening came, one of the chaps took a shovel and said that he was going to the woods to ease himself. We had bogs that we brought with us, but for some unknown reason, some of the chaps preferred to take a shovel, dig a hole, and hover over it.

A few minutes later, he came back and told me that he had found a body. I said, "*WHAT?* How could that be? Are you joking?"

He looked at me seriously, still with the shovel in his hand and said, "This is no joke, come and see."

I went with him down a small track, and then a few metres in the wood, he showed me what he had found. It was true. It was a body of a man. I went straight away and told my boss who got onto the German police, and later, the whole area was surrounded with German police cars and ambulance. At around 23.00 hrs the whole thing was cleared up, and that same time our main party went away, and left us as rear party. The night was black and foggy. There was only three of us left behind in this thick, dark and foggy forest. To tell you the truth, a frightening feeling came over me. One time the two other chaps had gone away doing the work we had to do, and I was left there all on my own. It was the same time when the Bader Meinhof group was active in Germany.

The landrover lights pierced through the thick fog, but behind it was horribly dark. Then I heard a sound, that made me jump, it was just one of the guys who had come back for something. When all three of us were finally together, sitting around the fire, and drinking tea, we found out that there was something wrong. One of us had to go through the forest for two miles to sort something out. I volunteered. I set out, and believe me, it wasn't an easy task, but I managed it, came back shattered and needing some rest. We finally left that forest and went to where the main party was. When we got there we heard all the news about the body that one of our soldiers had found. It was of a German who had been missing for some time.

The last day of the exercise was terrible, it was raining, and the place where we camped was awful. At about 16.00 hrs, we started packing up to go back to camp. When all was ready, again, the main party was off leaving us as rear party. We were always rear party anyway. We were wet and dirty, and I mean *really* wet and dirty. We finally set off from where we were camped, and drove for the autobahn. When we were coming up from our base, in the beginning, we were on the right side of the autobahn. Now that we were going back to our base, we were on the left, on the same side where we had earlier seen the drive in and those men working there. About fifty metres or more just before the entrance to the drive in, our landrover came to a halt, in a rather strange way. All the time it had been working perfectly. Traffic was very busy where the landrover halted. There was nothng at all that we could do.

An army ambulance came along and offered to tow us to the drive in. Our landrover just would not move. The army ambulance went on its way because there was nothing that it could have done. A German heavy duty truck came along and offered to do the same as the army ambulance without little success. The German police came and they too could not do anything, but they made sure that traffic flowed safely along. We had no phone on us so that we could phone back to base and fill them in with all that had taken place. We could only get back to base when our exercise camp was set up. So just as I was about to go and see if I could find a phone, a big German crane came along and hooked us up. It had trouble moving us. In the end, they managed to drag us in the drive way, but the wheels of the rover still refused to turn. There were tyre marks left on the autobahn.

We thank the chaps in charge of the crane, we locked up the rover and we went down a road just ahead of us. What we found funny was, that there were no one working in this driveway. The cabins were all locked up. We got down this road that we followed and came to a T junction. Straight ahead were two or three houses. We went to the first one. The door opened, and a woman was there. She saw us and went back in and came with some news papers. Only I was allowed to enter the house in the state I was in – *muddy boots.*

The woman had two daughters with her. I didn't see a man around. I explained to her in my not so good German what had taken place, and that I need to call my base. She allowed me to use her phone. I called base and let them know where we were and what had happened. They said we must wait where we are, and transport would come and pick us up. I must let you know that the landrover was not empty, it was laden down with drums and other materials. I went out the house after the phone call and joined the other two soldiers. We walked back up the road to the drive in and waited.

Late in the evening transport from our base turned up. A big roll on crane came along, you know the one with those big massive chains and cranes that lifts reasonable loads.

72

We were now on our way. Before we got into our base camp, one of the soldiers in our group said:

"You know what came into my head just now?"

I said, "No. What?"

He said, "I was thinking that that dead man's spirit must have taken you over."

I was amazed, I said, "That's *ridiculous*. What made you think that way?"

He said, " It's just the way things worked out. You ending up at that house, and the woman only let you in and no one else. As if she knew you were coming."

I told him that he was daft for thinking that way. "It's totally impossible for a spirit to take over another body. We're soldiers and we shouldn't be thinking such foolishness."

We left the German road and entered through the gate into our base camp.

It was nice to be back at camp. We were only in for two days, and out we went again, this time for one week. Wilhelmina must be thinking, I hardly get to see my hubby. But that was what this regiment was all about – exercise. For the three months we were in camp, we made the best of it.

*

Terry and family, Bill and Susan were soon to be leaving for England. Their army service was nearing its end. I had not long to do myself. I had a couple more athletic meetings to attend.

I was in fit shape and ready for the athletics meeting in England. This was an Inter Services meeting. The event I was in was the shot put. The guy who was number one for

England was there, a very big solid figure. It was nice to watch all the different styles in the shot put. Everyone gets to throw three times. My first put was lousy, just about 13 metres and some. I must do better I told myself. The English number one turn came. What a beautiful style of throwing. He hit the 20 metres target. When my turn came, I made it to 14 metres. It was impossible to beat the number one in England. When my last throw came, I hit 15 metres and 35cm. I was pleased with what I had achieved.

Back in Germany, we had a party for Terry and Trisha and Bill and Susan. It was held in camp and there was a great group playing. They turned out to be from the Netherlands. One of my soldiers keep telling the group that there's a lady here also from the Netherlands. The evening went down well, all had a good time.

The last summer camp we had was way down in Germany near to Trier. It was great. Even though we had to do some tough things daily, it still turned out well. At night, we had the time to ourselves to check out places.

The chaps, I thought, were mad, for they did something that was really crazy. Our camp was high up on the mountain overlooking the Geman town. We walked acoss a long bridge, then down a street leading to all the beer bars. The night was still young, and we seated ourselves in this bar, about six of us. We started out drinking beer when suddenly it turned to wine. When soldiers start to drink beer or wine, they're like beasts, but harmless. Our table was filled up with many wine bottles, and each bottle at that time, was costing around 50 German marks. I think what we had been drinking was Mosel wine. It had that kick while it was going down your throat, and if you're not careful, it could lay you out, there and then.

I got used to it after a while, and used to sling it down like water. This night while we were at the third bar, just off the road, in a side lane, I found myself alone at the table. The last thing I knew or heard, was they had gone to the wc. Then when I looked behind me out into the road, I saw these faces staring back at me, and beckoning me to come, with waves of their hands, and movements of their heads. I was absolutely lost and I didn't know what was going on. Staggering across the long bridge back to our campng place, I heard what they had done. They had left without paying the bill. I sobered up. How foolish, I said to them. Can't you see that I'm the only black one among you? The waitresses and barman would not forget that at all.

We got back to the camping place, and our tents were laid out in the muddy field next to the fence and the track leading down to the bridge. It was about 2 am when I heard the Mercedes car coming up the track. I said to the chaps that we are all in for it now. A few minutes later, the sgt major and some guards were there at our tents waking us up. We had to go out, and the German recognized us because of me, being black. We had to settle the business there and then, and back to our tent. What a foolish thing they had done.

We enjoyed the summer camp. On the last day, the tv from the area came and took some shots. In the evening we saw it in the main tent. With the summer camp over, we headed back to our base camp. It was a very long journey back.

A couple of weeks and Terry, Trisha, Bill and Susan would all be back in Blighty. As for myself I still had one more year left. And of course, one more athletic meeting. This was to be held in Aldershot. It was the Army Athletics meeting.

*

I entered for the 400 metres. I don't know if I was crazy or what, but I did board the plane to England. I remembered back in Singapore I had entered for the 400 metres running on tarmac. When the race had ended, I found myself rather weak in both my thighs, so I went in the shade on the grass to rest. After quite a long while, I felt a bit better. I was planning then to jack this 400 metres race in, but I was urged on by some others who were also going to England.

In the German stadium I did a lot of training. Every other day 600 metres. I really did my best. I had to be at my best to beat the reigning Army champion. I didn't know who it was until

I got to Aldershot. The guys kept on pointing to this other chap. They said, "That's him!" So I started making plans how to run the race.

It was a nice day. Many people were there to watch the race. It was a red cinder track – eight lanes. I started doing some short sprints, and lifting my legs, well my knees high in the air.

Then it was time to line up.

I must admit at first, I was a bit nervous. Quite a lot of things could go wrong in this sort of race. The timing had to be perfect, and I had listened carefully to my trainers. I know what I had to do. There on the line, waiting for the gun to go off, I let my eyes drift all around the track as if I was actually running. Then when my eyes hit a certain spot around the track, I knew exactly what I had to do.

The gun went off, and this was it. The race of the Army Athletics 400 metres final. I hit the track just as I was supposed to do. I was fit, I knew I was capable of causing upset. My feet hitting the track as I sped along. Then we came up to the last 200 metres. The Army champion was there just on my right easing down the last 100 metres. I was there beside him. I was talking to myself, *"Don't let him get away."* I called up some more effort, and was next to him. He hit the tape just ahead of me. He immediately turned around and shook my hands. My position was second. That wasn't bad at all. Later on I went out drinking with the guys, and the evening turned out be be quite enjoyable.

That then, was my last athletic meeting. I went back to Germany to my camp and got awarded with an army badge to put on the blazer. Terry, Trisha, Bill and Susan were now about to depart, and we sent them on their way as the custom was.

Back in the German village, I got on with quite a number of people. So many invitations that it was not an easy task to remember them all. I do remember that I was in the pub on a Wednesday – the one up on the hill. I was invited to this home of a millionaire who travelled a lot around Europe. Unfortunately, I didn't get the time to do so.

In the last year, a funny thing happened. The road I lived on was a very long road. At the end of this road, there was a big massive house there, and I learned later on that it was the commanding officer of our camp who was living there. Funny thing as well, it was one of our drivers, I mean from my troop, who had been picked to drive the commanding officer.

Time crept up slowly and let us know that we could no longer stay in the army. We had done our time, every one of us enjoyed it, even the wives and kids. But the army is not easy, anyone will tell you that. You have to be fit, able, courageous, and very much determined.

6

Back to Germany. End of Service

After Terry, Trisha, Bill and Susan left, I started planning my own departure. Seeing that I was going to take up residence in the Netherlands, I had to do a lot of running around and getting papers sorted out.

Leaving friends and people behind is one of the hardest things in life. But as we all know, families keep moving around. In the village where I lived there was a get together in the pub. And at work, well, you know what they'll do – give you a good send off. It was a busy time, very busy.

Handing over the place where we lived took up some time as well, and we finally got transport to take our stuff away. It is goodbye Germany, and here I come, well, here we come. Wilhelmina was from the Netherlands so that was no problem to her. It was I, I couldn't speak the language properly, for it was rather difficult to learn. I remember when I was back in England, knocking around Nottingham, I went into a bookstore and got a magazine. I saw on a page that you can learn different languages. There were quite a number of countries listed, but not the Netherlands. It was only now that I knew the answer.

Before I came out of the army, I already had a job in the Netherlands. It was with an agency to do odd jobs for one year. I had to drive a van around many different areas, picking up people and taking them to where we had to work, then I would take them back, and get home at 23.00 hrs.

I t was odd knowing now that you were free, and you can sleep in as long as you like. For a few weeks I felt strange. Well, no one came shouting and threatening me.

So I was really free.

*

I like the Dutch people. They have this way about them that for me was too easy going. Too relaxed sort of life. But it works for them. Everyone is allowed to do what ever they like as long as they do not break the law. I found though, that when a Dutchman gets angry, he does the most stupid thing that a human being can do. I notice too, the police were wearing guns in the street. Now I was really baffled. Why wear guns if the people were so friendly? Up to now, I still cannot answer that question.

We manged to get ourselves into a small flat but it was nice and cosy. Luckily for us, there was a school right across the road. And the shops weren't that far away, about 100 metres.

The first day at work was rather funny. I was working on this conveyor belt filling sacks with food for animals. It was hard work, and the rumbling and noise was if you were in a mad house.

Suddenly, the conveyor belt got jammed and the whole system shut down. One of the bosses came over and told me that I must not let that happen again. I have to work a bit faster, and not let the system shut down again. I looked across and saw the faces of some of the workers, they were glad every time the system shut down because it took some time to get it working again.

I worked at another place where six of us sat around a spinning table. There was this contraption where cans would come down from above us and unto the table. Beside us was a box with small stoppers, we had a hammer in our hands. When the cans hit the table that was spinning around, we took a stopper, place it in the small opening in the can, then we gave it a bang with the hammer. We began work about 8 am and didn't finish until 17.00 hrs. We had a lunch break for half an hour. One day I heard this young chap saying: "Ik zie het niet zitten." I didn't know what he meant until the lunch break came; and after the lunch break, I didn't see him again. I think he found it terrible just to sit there and knocking plugs in a can all day long.

There was one week when I picked up a student doctor and a psychologist. We all worked at a wood factory where they made lumber. It was very interesting to see how the machines worked. I was really amazed. I was at a conveyor belt where I had to sort out the good pieces of lumber from the bad. Then I had to take them to a machine that dried them. When it was lunch time, the student doctor, the psychologist and myself sat outside eating our lunch. I opened my lunch box and took out two slices of bread with cheese on them, then I sliced each piece in two. The psychologist said, "That's amazing, see how he sliced his bread in four pieces!"

I said, "Is there something strange about that?"

The psychologist said: "We can tell from how people slice their bread what sort of people they are."

I said to him, "Tomorrow, I shall slice my sandwiches into six pieces." Then he began to laugh.

I enjoyed working at the wood factory. I saw many things that I had not seen before, and I got to see how from the wood, all those different panels were made for the houses.

I tried to get a full time job at a Spaghetti factory, but because I was going away for a month, it did not happen. When I came back, I worked in a butter factory. This work was very dirty, outside in a shed, we had to melt butter that was sent back to the factory from other countries. What a smell that was; and the heat. Then we had to unload the lorries that came back from the continent or is going to the continent with pallets of different brand of butter. Then sometimes we had to clean up in the area where they were experimenting with the different butter. Then we worked in a place where they made sausages. I had to learn how to make them in this machine. One day there was a room where the flour is kept deep down in a sort of round container, and there was a contraption leading from it to the machines that would make the dough. We were sent to clean this container because it was almost empty. We went down these step ladders right down to the bottom.

While we were down there, suddenly we heard this great rumbling noise, and someone at the top shouting, *"COME ON! GET OUT QUICKLY."* The trucks had come with flour and automatically they were loading the container. Flour had already started pouring down when we just manage to get ourselves back to the top.

In the same building where the conveyor belt was, we had to load trays and trays of sausages and then take them into this frozen room. I tell you it was really cold and freezing. We had to put on special suit before we got in there. As soon as I got in, I wanted to get out straight away. One could hardly breathe. The door to this room was awfully thick and heavy. I remember one day someone close the door with my fingers beneath. When it was opened again, I dare not look down at my fingers, for I thought that they all had come off, but luckily, they were all still there, it was because of the cold that I did not feel much pain, but later, the pain came. Everything turned out ok in the end.

*

Then it happened. I actually got myself a *real* job. Of all the places, I ended up in a computer firm. They were making printers with the spin wheel system. They were also making table computers. I started out making the cables with plugs on both ends.

The big boss was from Canada. He got me in his office for a chat. He had a photo of his wife and two kids there on his table. The holder was red all around. He said to me, "If I said that that was green," pointing to the photo holder, "what would you say?"

I said, "I see red, and I'm sure everyone else would see red. It could be that something is wrong with your eyes." I then left the office after some more chat. Next day, instead of making cables, I was working just outside the administration office on a copy machine. There was a young beautiful blonde girl kept bringing out papers for me to copy.

After a few weeks working with that copy machine, they placed me in a group where I was the only man. They started teaching me how to repair bread-boards or I should better say that they were print boards that were placed in the spin-wheel printer. Even if it took a whole day to repair one board, it didn't matter at all. At least, when they put it into the machine, the printer started working.

I have to now tell you a story, one that is true, but rather strange.

When I was living back in Germany, in the village with the two pubs, I happened one night to see something rather strange. In my dream or vision, I saw this place where two trains arrive at the same time – one on the left, and the other on the right. I saw this building where I'm in a room and working beside a window, with the railway line in view.

It so happened that when I went for this job at the computer place. I came up from Nijmegen to a place called Wijchen. When the train stopped, on the opposite side, another train stopped as well. I got off the train and headed for the computer building. I went through the main door, and at the back in a corridor, there was a door straight ahead of me. We turned right and went through another door. One day, I happen with someone else to go to that door that I had seen on the way in. When the other person opened the door, I saw many iron bolders, in the room as if they were holding up the roof. No furniture was in the room, and no personnel.

A couple of months later, workmen, I heard were working inside that room. All the iron bolders were taken out, and chairs and tables and all sort of other furniture were placed inside.

I told you earlier that I was taken away from one job and placed with some women who were testing the electronic prints for the spin wheel printer. Well, I was seated at my own table, after I had been a while amongst those women, and had all the equipment beside me for testing the electronic prints. There was a window next to me, and a big yard where the trucks and cars were parked. Beyond that was the railway line leading from Nijmegen to Wijchen.

Exactly what I had seen in the dream or vision is what actually took place in that room where I had been busy working. Could you imagine what I was thinking to myself? It wasn't the first time that I had these strange dreams or visions. The soldiers whom I had worked with back in Germany and Singapore knew all about them.

When I first arrived in Singapore, I had a dream or a vision of a beach with many people on it. I stood up and looked out to sea and started shouting, *"THEY'RE NOT COMING ACROSS THIS SEA."*

Later, I found out that the British were thinking that the enemy would be coming across the sea, and made plans to stop them. But the enemy actually came through that thick jungle.

Then all the numbers of the Singapore Lottery came to me, and in the morning, I could only remember four numbers. All day long I was trying to remember the other two without any luck. I had told my Staff Sergeant about it and gave him the numbers. He won quite a lot of money.

I don't know what it was with me, but I kept on getting these dreams or visions, and they came often. One time we were on an exercise on a big mountain. I went to sleep the first night we arrived there. I woke up the next morning remembering clearly, all the details. When I went to breakfast, I told the chaps about it, they all started laughing because what I had told them, sounds impossible.

I told them that I had seen my Staff Sergeant stuck with his landrover, and I had to go and pull him out, then I, in my landrover also got stuck. I told them that I saw all the 3 ton wagons with their trailers going down a hill, and they all rammed into each other, and couldn't go away.

It snowed and the area we were in was awfully snowy and muddy. Exactly what I had seen with my Staff Sergeant happened, and me myself, in the landrover, got stuck and I had to be pulled out.

When the order came for us to pull out for another location, all the wagons were lined up on this great slope, it was icy, and there was a great ditch at the left-hand side of the road. It so happened that as they started out, the wagon at the rear was jack-knifed by its trailer and caused all the others in front to slide over in the ditch. Each wagon had a trailer behind it. So there it was, just as I had seen it the night before.

A day or two just before that incident, I went alone through the woods until I came to a ridge overlooking a deep drop. It was a nice sunny day, and I made myself comfortable against a tree. The lads all knew where to find me in case there were problems. I must have fell asleep or something. For I had seen these soldiers coming up the hill towards me. But when I came to my real self, the hill was empty. There were no soldiers climbing up. I must have fallen asleep and dreamt. Later, I heard that there was a great battle fought on this mountain. How odd!?

I have given you the first part of me getting a job in Wijchen in a computer firm, and about the things that I had seen which came to pass. Now I shall tell you some more.

Back in Germany, before I came to the Netherlands, I saw a great field, unprepared and full of weeds. Then I saw houses, and car parks. I saw this orange car parked in one of the car parks.

While working at the computer firm, I got the chance to see if I could get a place to live in Wijchen. One day some family of Wilhelmina took us to a place where the local Gemeente were planing to build some new houses. We went and had a look. When I got there, I said to them that the first will be built here, pointing to the spot, and I would be living in it. They all looked at me as if I was mad.

After a while, we went back and had a look. Building had begun, there were already the beginnings of many buildings. And of course, the one that I said I would be living in, was the first one to be completed. And I am not telling you any lies, the first house was given to us, and there were big celebrations. There were even news about it in the local papers.

We moved from Nijmegen and settled in our brand new house. After some time I had some dream or vision of a great house with a strange top and when one walked through the main door, on the left was a sort of entrance like a tunnel. You are not going to believe this, but this community house had not yet been build. There were no plans for it yet. Later on, the workers started construct- tion, and would you believe it, when the community place was finished, it was exactly as I saw it in the dream or the vision.

Later on, I bought this second hand car which was orange, and when I parked it in the car park just outside our new home, I couldn't see the back wheels. Just as how it was in the dream. But I thought something was wrong, so I went and check and found that it was the way that the park was built made the car looked as if it had no back wheels. Very funny!

I must go back to just before I came out the army, to tell you something that was rather strange.

I had a vision or a dream. I saw this Irish chap in his communications truck, and as I came forward, there was an attack from the enemy. The Irish soldier (he was in the British army) fell down dead and I saw lots of sparks flying all over the place.

Then I saw soldiers at a sort of sea-port, and they started marching on a sort of sloping ground, and then out in the country side. Miles out, they came to the enemy who were very young. These young chaps started crying.

Then I saw a great ship, and a sort of plane from the enemy came and bombed it. From the explosion, I saw so many multi-coloured strange things. Then I heard a voice telling me to tell Mrs Thatcher to get the ships ready ... then I woke up.

I went around for some time didn't know what to do, and this was because no one took me seriously. And not only that, the message "Get the ships ready!" Did it make any sense?

It was only while I was working at the computer place that I heard the news of the Falkland war, and how for the first time, the enemy had used some sort of bomb to bomb a ship. And that the soldiers had a long march over the mountains where they met up with the enemy who were very young and were crying for their mothers.

So then, I kept receiving all these dreams or visions and I had to keep them all to myself. And I also found that every single thing that I was told, came to pass.

Like I was told that Paul Mc Cartney would come out best from the Beatles. It was only when I had a dream or a vision of England becoming a state of America that I started wondering what the hell is going on here. The fact that I could not see such a thing happening.

I saw soldiers invading our country, and I was there, but not part of it. I saw these soldiers all in grey uniform defending the country. I found this odd, because I didn't see any other uniform. Then after some weeks I came to the conclusion that it was the Royal Air Force who were defending the country along with a few other soldiers. That is really strange. I then decided to keep all this stuff to myself and not let anyone laugh at me.

*

I am back at the computer place and everything is working out fine. I am enjoying my work, and I get along well with all the other workers.

Then suddenly, I am taken away to another room where there are many table computers and printers. They started teaching me how to build up the table computers and how to test them. At that time, each computer had at least 10 bread boards inside. I wasn't accustomed to all this technical stuff, but I was enjoying it. After they had taught me everything, they then left me to get on with it.

Computers and printers had to be tested by me, and then next door a man would come and take them away and pack them up, ready to be shipped to Denmark, Sweden, Germany, Norway, and all other places who had placed orders.

At this time, not thinking about how I really felt, I just kept on concentrating on my work. There were a lot of pressure around. Then they started teaching me about CPU's and how they are made up. Was I really thinking that one day all this information could really blow me? Well, it did. My head burst (not literally!) I just wasn't myself. I went haywire like a mad man.

For a few weeks I rested and slowly came to, and to the realization of what had happened to me. Thank God I was ok! But the family side wasn't. It went down the drain. Things were really bad in that area. It was like a treasure that you know you were losing. Trying to save it. But we do learn from our mistakes.

Wilhelmina and I got divorced, and I moved back down to Nimegen, staying in a hotel, waiting to find myself a flat. I had registered with the housing people some time back, and all I had to do now is wait. It was costing me quite a lot of money staying at that hotel. Wilhelmina and the kids came to visit quite a number of times.

Someone told me that if I want to get out this hotel, I must get onto the phone and harass the housing people. They'll get fed up with me, and then find me some place to live. It worked.

One day I was out walking, I came back earlier than usual. I stepped into my room and saw the cleaner kneeling down over my suitcase which was open. When she realized that I was present, she got up and left the room.

There was a girl in the same street living on the other side who tried to make friends with me. Sometimes she'll meet me at the town's square, and we'll just chat for hours. She told me that her ceiling was nothing but mirrors.

I finally got a call from the housing people. They told me that they have a place for me. I went to see it and took it straight away. The rent was ok, better than staying in that hotel.

I had no job and busied myself trying to find one. Every night I stayed in and went out daily for little walks. One night there was entertainment in the town for four days. I decided I shall go and have a look and then come back. I was standing against a rail. On my left there was a stage where a band was busy playing. Straight ahead of me were people sitting on chairs. I saw this woman staring at me all the time. The trouble is, she had a man sitting next to her. That put me off straight away. But I still kept on looking at her. After about two hours she got up and made her way exactly to where I was standing, then walked away.

A week later, I actually bumped into that same girl while I was going into a shop. For some unknown reason I gave her the nickname of "Eyes."

The first thing I said to her was, "Have you got a boyfriend. Are you married.?"

She said that she was married, and that she like me. I told her that I do not go around with people who are already attached.

After two years living in my little flat with only one table and two chairs, I decided to go to a place and start learning

Dutch seriously. There I met this teacher and something sparked between us. She had two children – a boy and a girl. The relationship only lasted for three years. I was back on my own.

Looking around for jobs, I decided to go to the high school and see if they'll take me on. My luck was in. They needed a helper in the reproduction area, copying books for the students. They asked me to start in the coming New Year and I did so. Another full time job, this was just too great.

There were quite a lot of students in this school; and the number of teachers were very high.

Out in the corridor, I saw the old man who I was going to work under, down on his knees, and rolling this paper on this old contraption, to get what they call a copy, so that they could print it many times, and then hand it out to the teachers and students. I was thinking to myself, 'this is old fashion. Something has to be done about this.' I had to be careful as well, not to go round pushing my weight. I started liking the work, even though it was hard. I had also told myself to switch off, and not to get involve with none of the girls, of course you can communicate, but keep your distance. Knowing the Dutch, it wasn't that easy. The Dutch are always close, one big family. So it was hard to completely switch off. And being British disciplined, it was very hard as well. I used my discipline, tolerated the Dutch system, and carried on with my work.

Later on, more students began to enrol at our school from all parts of Germany. Soon, the school was really big, it was international. That mean we in the reproduction area had to make more books and print more daily news.

We got new printing machine that were first class – a joy to work with.

There's one thing I just couldn't stand. One day we were playing football against the women, and the coach kept on saying to me, "Give them the ball, and let them score."

Inside of me was tightening up. I wanted to cry out. We don't do that back in England. If the women are good enough then they'll beat us. But asking the men to pretend and let the women win was not on. But I kept it all cool and did what the head coach said.

The first year went down well. I didn't go away for holidays, I stayed at home. The following year I did go to England. Then I had the chance to go up to King's Cross Station, and then to take a train down to Nottingham. I knew the address and telephone numbers of both Terry and Bill, so I decided to give them a surprise visit.

Terry and Trisha, Bill and Susan were all pleased to see me. Their children were growing very fast. We went to the centre of the town one day, and we all had milkshakes. I was only down for a couple days, then I went back to London where I had been staying.

I like London a lot, there are many things to do there. I like to walk around, looking at all the buildings, and walk through the parks and all the arcades filled with expensive stuff – but that didn't worry me. I also like to quickly slip in a coffee place and relax for a bit. One of the things I really like is to walk around in safety. Of course, in any big city, there's always some sort of trouble. Maybe I was lucky, but I walked around peacefully and didn't bump into any trouble. I even went into Harrod's and looked around. That place was nice to visit, but it was not for the likes of me.

I visited the National gallery and looked around for quite some time. I saw a massive painting which stretched from one corner of the room to the next. It was by Rembrandt, and I think it was called *The Night Watch*. I don't know much about painting or art, but my eyes would gaze at something that holds my interest.

I was very pleased with this job at the high school, but I was amazed that I managed to hold out for so long. I kept myself out of trouble; and I gave all that I had in me without holding back.

7

Going into retirement

Coming back over to the Netherlands from England with the boat was a great experience. I had to travel from Liverpool Street Station and up to where the boat was. It took about three hours and some to get to the port just outside Rotterdam.

I am now going to tell you something that actually happened to me while I was on the ship. You must know by now that I'm always going through some strange experiences. This one is absolutely true.

I have no need to tell any lies here.

I was on a Catamaran ship, a strange sort of ship that was sailing on top of the water. On this trip, I forgot to book myself a seat. All the seats were taken and so I found myself sitting on a sort of bench right at the back on the left-hand side. There, I could see the water from the ship pouring out in a stream behind the ship. There was no one else on the bench but myself. Then suddenly, she was there, sitting next to me on the left – Princess Diana. She had on some blue faded jeans, a white shirt, and a small black watch on her left hand. Just like the picture that was in one of the daily papers in England.

I knew it was her, and I kept quiet. I am like that. When strange things happen, I just take it all in, keep it to myself for some time, then I would let it out. Many people reading this would think that I have lost my marbles, but I know what I'm writing is true.

The Princess spoke first, and being in a sort of shock state, I hardly spoke, but I manage to ask her where she was living. She told me Amsterdam. This happened around the end of July. I always come back from England a week before I had to go to work. So I had a whole week to rest at home. We go back to work around the 8th August, but the teachers and the students don't start until the first week in September.

When something like what happened to me, happens to you, it is very hard to tell people about it. So I had to go around with it, and thinking "how could that happen?"

*

Well, I still settled down and concentrated on my work. The teachers would bring material for you to make a book for the students. It had to be done properly without any mistakes. But some times the printing machine skips a page, and gives us something to think about. Other times, the teachers bring lots of books where we have to copy certain pages, then put them together to make a book. I think that one can go bonkers if they are not well prepared for that sort of work. We had a few printers that were very reliable. From 08.00 till 18.00 hrs they were there making all that noise – printing.

That first year at the school in July, many people from all over the world came to walk in the festival called *"The four days marches."* I was walking through the town when this car, a small one, came along and accidentally went up on the side walk and touched the shoes of a big well built man. The man turned and went to the car with the intention of dragging the driver out of the seat. I went between the two of them, with both my arms sprawled across the car. The chap in the car apologized but the big man started smashing with his hands against the glass of the door. All the time, I'm there, but he did not hit out at me. Then the chap in the car managed to drive away with his window shattered.

It wasn't very long before I found myself in a relationship with a woman from London. So I spent my holidays in London every year. I enjoyed it all. It was like on a another planet. It is strange that when I was young and back home, I used to hear all the talk about London, now I was actually seeing it for myself. I did see bits of it when I was in the army.

Every year in July buses came to take the teachers and the personel to some place in the Netherlands. We either went to some festival or to a museum. Sometimes we go and make a picknick of it.

Other times we would be riding bicycles for over 30 kilometres with a map. Another time we ended up in Friesland. Where we stayed, someone said that we have to walk to the sea. I hadn't been to the sea for a long time,and I was pleased that we were going there. We started out, climbing sandy hills, and then down them, and then up them; and still no sea was to be seen. But after a while, it was there. The day was hot, but I knew that the water would be cold. I was planning just to dip my foot in, but I think, I can't remember if I did went in for a dip. The whole thing was very enjoyable.

The old boss of mine went on pension and left me all alone in the reproduction area. It was hard going then. I kept everything in order until later a young married girl came to join me. She was very stubborn, but kind and loving.

The first funeral I had to go to in all the places I've worked, was here. A young teacher got killed while driving to Africa. I was really sad as we all gathered in the church that was just next door.

I've never been in that church before. I've heard people talked about it. While I was seated close to the front with the coffin not far away, I noticed something that was on the right of the pulpit. It was the sign of the Ram – the first astrological sign of the zodiac. Now that left me really baffled. I sat there wondering why the first sign of the zodiac was in a church.

Ok! I had to attend two more funerals – one of a Polish woman, and the other of an old concierge. I know that it is part of life and we all have to go through such things. I remember way back I used to visit this 84 year old woman who lived in the town, not far from the center. Every time I entered her room, I was thinking, *"Oh! God, I hope she doesn't offer me any coffee."* Have you ever had coffee from an old dear? I did take a cup from her one time, and I almost spit it out straight away, but manage to drink it down, and I think she saw how I frowned my face. She was a nice woman, kind and helpful. She loved children as well.

I used to ask her lots of questions about how she felt now being old. She kept saying to me, "I want to go away. I don't like it any more." The old woman passed away later on. I went to her funeral and for one whole week, I felt strange. I felt really down. Later on, I felt good again.

I went to another funeral of a woman I knew for many years, a very wonderful cook. She had me hooked on her home made soup. She was the mother of Wilhelmina. It's amazing how many people you meet up with at a funeral. There were some who I didn't really want to meet and end up talking to them. We were in this specially built place where the coffin goes through the fire. And then ashes are given to the family.

I also found myself in a special building. I went to see Wilhelmina grandmother on her mother's side who had passed away. They showed me the room she was in. I went in and stood there looking at her with all sort of thoughts passing through my head. Not long ago, I had been talking to her, now she is lying here all dressed up waiting to be taken away.

I already said to myself long time ago, there are many things that I do not understand, and I will not ask any questions about them unless it is very important. If I have to go to war, I will go to war. If I have to get married, I will get married. If the marriage end, then there's nothing I can do. But if there's no war, I'll enjoy the peace as much as I can.

The last funeral I've been to was that of Wilhelmina's mother. Then things went back to normal. Well, normal for me, but for others, they were still attending funerals, and that is something that is always with us.

Things were going pretty well in the reproduction area. Another woman joined us and she was a Capricorn, and I knew straight away what was going to happen. And it did just like I had guessed. It didn't take her long to get herself in a high position. I was glad for her, she was a nice person. But Capricorns would trample over their own mothers in order to get to the top. That is a fact.

*

Every year on holidays, I found myself in London. And from there I would visit Nottingham. And of course meet up with Terry and his family and Bill and his family. We would all exchange news. We would gossip about what's been going on in Nottingham and in Nijmegen.

They were building a big massive complex to house our school. Many students keep coming to our school, and it was not big enough to house them. The building we were in was old. We started preparing ourselves for the big move. It was going to be my last year in that old building.

I worked with the young married girl for ten years. The relationship with that woman in London came to an end. We still kept in touch now and then. Just before the school left to go holidays the moving men came in and began moving things out.

I went on holidays.

When I came back it was the new year. I was now wearing a uniform for the first time. The new school complex I reported to was big. It was nice, unbelievable. I lost my way a few times going from one place to the next. It took me quite a while to find out where things were – all the different departments.

There were now four of us working in the reproduction area. Some fantastic printing machines were there, a colour printing one as well. The book binding machine was great. I love the place. You get that feeling of being very happy in your work.

I only had now seven months left before I would again be on holiday, this time for a long time. My service for pension would then be ended.

I enjoyed the few months I had left at the new school complex. Things went fine. Then the time came for me to say *Goodbye*.

*

It was in the month of July and a going away party was arranged for me. My children and grandchildren came. And the reception went down well. Then the boss, who was a woman, had a taxi arranged for me to take me away.

That was it then, I don't have to work any more.

It is strange when you wake up and knowing that you don't have to worry. You don't have to rush and catch the bus for work. You can stay as long as you like in bed. As for me, I'm disciplined, and I don't want to play lazy. I always get up in the morning and have breakfast, and then go to the town.

This July then, found me on the train and I was off to London. Before, I used to go by boat, but now I took another route, under the tunnel from Brussels to Waterloo. Later, it changed to King's Cross Station. I enjoyed every bit of it. Going through the tunnel didn't take long at all, just twenty minutes; felt a bit cold that's all.

When I came back from holidays, I started making plans

to go and stay in London for six months. I knew that it was going to cost some money, especially staying in London. I found a nice flat not far from the tube station with quite a lot of amenities around. It was great. Just across the road from where I stayed, was a shop, the people were from overseas. When I first entered the shop, the man said to me, "I knew you would come." I didn't say anything. When I got back to the flat, I started thinking over what the man had said. Then I knew what he meant.

Although the flat was nice, it was high up. I was already making plans in case a fire should break out, what steps I would take. Not far from me was the Holiday Inn hotel. I saw something strange over that hotel. It wasn't a plane nor was it a helicopter. I have never seen anything like it before. I know what I'm saying because I have worked on many airfields and know what planes and helicopters looks like. Fighter planes and anything like that.

The windows of this thing was strange, round, and low. I noted down the time, and I did make a chart of it.

*

Back in Nijmegen, the month is February. I went shopping, and as I was walking along, I saw this shop with crystals and all sort of other stones in the window on show. I stepped in to have a look, started chatting with the sales woman, we became friendly. She had a boyfriend who was from another country. She also had two kids – two boys.

I met her boyfriend and we shook hands and chatted. I made sure that I kept my distance, still being friendly, but not to step out of line. Her boyfriend wanted to stay in the

Netherlands but was having problems. Four years I chatted with them. Her boyfriend could not stay any longer, having no permission to do so, they left the Netherlands.

Two years later, I went into a shop to buy a new pot, and there was a woman in the shop who lived in the same place where I lived. We always chatted on the bus when she was going down to start her work; and me going down to do shopping on certain days. She was a nice woman, very sociable and friendly and was married with one small daughter.

I started doing some experiments. For two long years I started reading by bible, kept away from women, drink and foolishness. Then I felt strange every time I went down to the town. I felt that I was above every one else, at the same time, I felt really good, but I didn't like the feeling of being above everyone else. So I gave up the whole thing – not completely. Now and then I would read the bible.

*

I'm back on the normal track, and I feel good about it. I see all the different human beings with their different problems. I see the town when there's a festival on, I go and have a look. I don't want any one to come and scare the living daylights out of me. I haven't had that for a long time, and I want to keep it that way. There are so many things that nature can do to us to make us cringe. I'd rather know before hand what's coming, and get out the way, and let it pass, then get on with what I have to do.

The woman who I talked with on the bus got herself another job but she didn't like it. She was trying hard to get herself a job in a school. For years I talked with her.

She finally got a job in a school near to where her daughter goes to school. So our chat on the bus has ended. When I'm at the bus stop, and she is coming back from taking her daughter to school, she always stop and chat.

The following year I met up with a friend and its gone two years now since we've been chatting and exchanging views. Since I'm not working any more, I got time to pursue my hobbies which are many. I listen to classical music – blues, jazz, rock, you name it. If it sounds good to me, I'll listen to it.

Talking about books, I'm just mad. But I realize that it is not possible to do all that you want to do in one lifetime. I like to go out eating in restaurants, that cost money as well. I like to travel a lot. I like to visit places that has no trouble and are peaceful and welcoming to its outsiders.

I love peace, but this is something that is really beautiful. It is deep within oneself, and sometimes it's hard to try to explain this feeling. Outside and around you there's always turmoil, but that is something we have to live with.

One of my hobbies is the research on the workings of astrology. I"ve been doing that now for over 40 years. I've read that the scientist has trouble finding out how it works. That is strange, because I have no trouble at all. But for those who believe in the bible, they need to read carefully what the Creator did on the fourth day.

Someone asked me today, do I belive in extraterrestrials. I had to answer yes even though I might be wrong. I did so because I find it hard to believe that we are the only one in all the great Universe. I do believe in the opposite side which is spiritual.

Life is precious and we should try and live it in a good

way. Of course, at times things would go wrong. But one shouldn't give up as soon as things go wrong.

I like reading about the ancient peoples. They were clever and set us on the road to many discoveries. They weren't far off when they said that the year was 365.25 years.

I think that we should try and get back on the right road – whatever that road might be. I got the strong feeling that we are on a road leading to destruction, if we don't stop and get on the right one.

Is there a right road? *Yes, there is.* And I don't have to say anything. You yourselves can see that it is so. You can still enjoy yourselves by being on the right road. Of course there are some potholes in it. You will see them and avoid danger.

I was reading some poetry from Lucretius. This is what he wrote:

"Anyone who fear death should consider the time before he was born. The past infinity of pre-natal non-existence; it is as though nature has put a mirror to let us see what our future non-existence will be like. But we do not consider not having existed for an eternity before our births to be a terrible thing; therefore, neither should we think not existing for an eternity after our death to be evil."

I am on my way home after buying a couple of books. The titles are:

"A Brief history of everyone who ever lived" by Adam Rutherford.

The other is: *"A Day in the Life of the Brain"* by Susan Greenffield.

Some heavy books, don't you think so?

I am at the station waiting to get the bus that goes my way. Suddenly, I see this girl on my left. I thought she too was waiting for her bus. She came closer to me and asked: "Do you want some money? What would you have done if someone had asked you that? I said to her, "I don't need money, I have enough." Then she carried on, "Do I need this ... do I need that ...?" Then my bus came, and I left her there.

Early in the morning I'm at the bus stop – I'm *always* at the bus stop – I need to go somewhere. No, seriously, I'm going shopping. I looked across the road to a pole standing there. There's no traffic coming from the left or the right. I'm thinking to myself to run across and touch that pole. Then again, why should I do that? But I *can* do it if I want. What is stopping me? Go on, *do* it!

I'm still standing there staring at it. You must by now think that I'm a nutter, well I'm not. I just like to think. And I do think about things quite often.

When I was young and I was waiting for the fishermen to come in with their boats full of all sorts of fish, I would drift off thinking about nature, life, dogs and cats and human beings. I think I must have been about nine years old when I start to think about why should a human should die before his cat or dog. It didn't make any sense to me. From that time onwards, I told myself not to think about it.

I started reading a book about Plotinus, the ancient Greek philosopher. He had his own spiritual system, the *one*, he would say was over everything. Then there was intelligence, and then the soul. He said that all existence came from these three. He had a hard time trying to find out if the soul is in the body or above it, and yet being part of it. I had a hard time trying to understand Plotinus. In the end it came out okay.

*

I like philosophy, but when I came to a book by Arthur Schopenhauer with the title of *The World As Will And Representation*, I began to think that I'm on the wrong road. I struggled through this book – reading and not really understanding – what it was all about. I put it down, then took it up later, and started reading it slowly.

One of my favourite books of course is the Bible. When I tackled Ezekiel, that was hard, interesting, especially his visons of God.

I like to watch a good game of football. In fact, I like to watch sports very much, no matter what it is. But I enjoy being in the sunshine and watching a good cricket match.

I'm absolutely crazy about music. I could listen to it all day. That's what I do actually. I start out with some classics, then some Irish songs by Cathy Ryan. Then rock and roll, and jazz and other stuff. I'm filled up every day with music.

I have great respect for every country with their own way of life. When I first came from the West Indies to Britain, their way of life attracted me very much. I was brought up in it from my youth. But what attracted me most was the three-class system – high, middle and low. I had no problem with that. Life was good knowing that it was so. Jupiter is much bigger than the earth, and we on earth know that Jupiter is the biggest planet in our solar system. So then, someone who is in a higher position than me, gets my respect. I had no problem with the system, it was there every day facing me, one could not get rid of it because that's the way it was.

I got stuck on classical because I had a girlfriend who was a painter and loved classical music. Now I'm listening to Tchaikovsky, Vivaldi and all the other greats. I didn't know anything about the painters, then suddenly, I had most of the names in my head.

I bought a CD some time ago, and it's only now I start listening to it. It is from Sweet, their greatest hits from the 70's, and believe it, I'm there jigging to the music, the music is sweet indeed. Another CD I'm listening to is by Trisha Yearwood, *Inside Out* a great CD.

*

I'm in my 42nd year studying astrology as my hobby. I have come to the conclusion that it has something definitely to do with us. It is hard to explain due to the fact that human beings are so unpredictable.

I know that astrology is true, and I'm amazed that the scientists can't find out why it works. The reason why I know it is true is because I see it in some of the faces. Some shows it more than others. And if you should ever see me on the streets, I'm always looking at people deeply, and I have to be careful because they might find it strange. But mean no harm by doing so.

Everyone of us has a record of things that has happened to us sometimes with no explanation. And things that has happened to us that is kept as a secret. If I'm drunk and I go into a fight and I get beat up, whose fault was it? I'm going to relate to you some strange things that has happened to me.

8

Some strange things

I went into town and popped into a mobile shop hoping to buy a new one. I had a shoulder bag which I placed beside me on the ground to take something out my pocket. Then I walked out of the shop, hopped on the bus; and about two minutes into the drive, I realize that I hadn't my shoulder bag with me. I started stamping like a little kid who has lost its toy, and I was shouting to the top of my voice, *"STOP THE BUS! STOP THE BUS!*

The driver stopped the bus, opened the doors and I rushed out the bus and there was by bag still in the same place where I had left it. What a relief that was.

Someone heard I was going to London, but I have been there many times before, told me to watch out and take care. I travelled from Brussels in belgium to Waterloo Station. Then from there I was on a bus going to my destination. Suddenly, the driver said that we have to change bus. I got my luggage and my small travelling bag and came to where the driver was. I put the bag down beside me, talked to the driver, and went out the bus leaving my hand bag. I never saw it again. I phoned all the places in connection with the bus I was on, and even went to the depot where lost goods were left. But I did not get my bag.

*

I'm in the Netherlands in the town. I went to get some fish. I had this small traveller's bag where you can put all your stuff in. I opened it up, took the wallet out and paid. Then I left without putting the wallet back in. I went out the shop. I went to do my normal shopping. Then I realize I hadn't had my wallet with me. I don't normally fear for anything, but this time, a certain fear came over me. Inside my wallet was my money and my passport. I rushed back to the fish shop, and as I walked in, the owner was smiling at me and showing me my wallet. Was I pleased?

Ever since then I became more careful and making sure that my wallet was on me and not in any bag.

You won't believe it! Remember I told you about that girl who came up to me at the station while I was waiting for my bus? Well, I'm in the middle of the town waiting for my bus home. There on my right, she was. I learn from her that she was a Christian. I said to her, "So that's why you wanted to help people. But I don't need no help at the moment."

I must admit I'm dressed as if I was someone needing help badly. As if I was down and out. I was not down and out. Of course, I'm old but still breathing the breath of life until ...

That girl started telling me a few things, and I stood and listened, and as my bus pulled in, she grabbed a piece of paper and wrote on it and gave it to me. On the bus, I looked at the paper and there was her name and her phone number.

I bumped into someone from the Jehovah's witness. I spent the whole afternoon with him because if he had convinced me, I would have become a member, but he failed to convince me.

There was one time I was busy looking at the sites around Piccadily Circus when I was surrounded by 5 young chaps just on the corner. I was amazed because this has never happened before. They were all English. They started being funny with me. But when they heard that I was an ex-soldier, they left me alone.

There was I on my bicycle going to work. It was early morning, a bit foggy. I was on the bicycle track with a road on my right. I was almost in the middle of the crossing when I saw lights coming from my right. It is strange what I did, for when the car hit the bike, I was on the ground. The bicycle was a write-off. The ambulance came and took me to the main hospital, then I was released later on.

I was coming back from England to Vlissingen. I think I was below on one of the decks where the bunks were free; there were four in one space. I was in the top bunk of the first two near to the door. I was fast asleep when strange things started happening Someone was shouting that the boat was sinking. Suddenly, it all went dark, then lights start flickering. I stayed put in my bunk, then this woman came in and took the bunk on the top of the next two that was much away from the door. I said to her that she couldn't stay there. She said: "Who said so?" I kept my mouth shut after she made herself comfy. I was forgetting that the place was free to anyone. Things went back to normal, and the ship wasn't sinking.

I was in this automatic washing machine place. The first wash was over and I was now waiting for the drying machine. This tall man came in sat beside me, he too, was waiting for his clothes to dry.

He started talking to me and the conversation went to Vietnam. He was a soldier there. The way he told me the story, I thought I was actually there and experiencing what he was telling me. He said at one place, it was very dark, and they had been waiting for some time for the enemy. Neither of them would make a move. Then he said one of them with a flame blower started it off. The enemy was there, quite a lot of them. He said the screaming was terrible. He also told me how the helicopter came in one after the other to ferry men away. I do like to hear or read about war stories and heroes, but this one was tough.

I was reading Ovid, and I got really interested about *Phaeton*. It seems to me that this story was about the sun travelling in its path – the ecliptic. Phaeton had told his friends that the sun was his father so they laughed at him. He went back and asked his mother if it was true. She said yes it was, and that Phaeton should go and find out for himself, which he did. He got to where the sun god was and asked to drive the sun chariots. The sun god was afraid but later he let Phaeton drive the sun horses, giving him instructions. The horses were so wild and fast that phaeton could not control them. He went off the path, fell to the earth setting it on fire.

I always dig in to these old stories to see what I could find. I got a couple more chapter to go to finish the *Twelve*

Caesars. Interesting reading, but horrible things those Emperors did. It is as if someone had made up the story, but it actually happened.

Ever since I had that vision about the roof of a house falling on my head, I'm thinking, 'What's going on?' I was there with a group of people, suddenly, we heard planes overhead. There was a long house with people in it. They were calling us to come quickly to safety. As we ran to the house with the weapons, the house collapsed. I felt a lot of things on my head.

I was working in a butter factory in the Netherlands when I met this man who told me a lot about the Japanese attack on Singapore.

Later, I looked up to see what actually happened and found that the Japanese did attack Singapore on the 8th December 1941 at 04;30 am.

Now what I find strange is that I wasn't born as yet. Because I am now researching astrology, I found out that my conception took place in December 1941.

The strange thing is: my mother told me that I was born with a caul.

I was now trying to make some sort of connection with reincarnation. The trouble is: I don't really believe in it. I believe that the cycle has to finish, so that all the generations could come through.

And of course, the possibility of spirits taking over the body. But how can they do that? I think it is possible.

I heard once a story about some army soldiers who were in their trucks and heading for a mine field, when suddenly, the driver saw another soldier in front his truck, didn't know where he came from. They were guided out of the mine field with no harm coming to any one of the trucks or the soldiers. Then the soldier just disappeared.

When I was young, I used to go to the cinema which was about 4 kilometres away. The cinema was always packed. When it was over, I would go outseide and look for people who was headed in my direction. Straight after the cinema was finsihed, all the light would go out, and the whole place became black like hell.

Sometimes I would find a couple of people going my way, and suddenly they depart and leave me all alone. There was the anglican church there on my left with its gates closed, and line from the gates down to the church steps with palm trees on both sides, and of course, graves were all there too.

When I was young, I was really afraid of the dark. Anyway, what I would do if no one was going my way? I would start running, and I won't stop until I reach my door.

I got a strong feeling that through the planetary com-binations which gives energies to mankind, certain people can get cosmic power. And I do believe that the *'Spirit'* is more powerful than any material thing.

I am doing some research work on what we call intercepted signs in astrology. These are signs that are not at the doors of the 12 houses. They have to wait their turn before they can take over.

So if we had the sign Taurus on the second door with the intercepted sign of Gemini in the second house, it means that Gemini has to wait until Taurus reaches its 30 degrees before it can take over.

So we have the intercepted sign of Gemini in the second house and I am trying to find out what it all mean.

I remembered the time when I went to watch some chaps playing cards. There were six of them. The game was *Three Cards Brag*. It's a game where you can bluff but you have to be clever doing so.

I learn the game quickly for the stakes at that time was 10 Pfennig. Later it went up to ten marks. Out of the six of us two was left, another and myself.

I had the cards there on the table, no one can see what they were. The other chap just won't give up. He kept on and on. He even put in his pay that he had to take home to his wife.

At the end he had a royal flush, while I laid out the three threes on the table. I felt very sad about the affair when later, some of the chaps told me that the chap was married and had three kids. I said he took the chance and he lost.

*

There are two things I'm always thinking about – they are time and sleep – and they are very strange. Time no one knows as yet what it is. Sleep, you dump yourself on the bed, and suddenly, you've gone away into some deep sleep and dreaming your head off. What is sleep really? And why do we have to sleep? I know people been researching to find out, but no proper answer has come to us.

I was there one time looking at the sea, then I saw a fish swimming along merrily. Then suddenly I thought of the way we human beings fight against each other, and killing, while the fish is still alive. I was looking for an answer. I think it was foolish to think that way and yet, it made some sense.

*

114

I got the shock of my life a couple days ago. I was just about to get on the bus to go home when this police van pulled up, came to the bus door, and said, *"You! Out!"*

I stood there speechless with my shopping bag in my hand. I stepped back out the bus. "Where did you come from?" One of the policemen asked me. I still was in shock and speechless. Then I manage to point with my left hand and said to them, "From that road over there." The woman bus driver wanted to go but I still looked at her asking to stay. The policemen said that they were looking for someone. Then they let me go to my bus. I thought to myself, "Who was this someone? Did he look like me? Why *me*?

But I've found out and knew all along that things happen to me that I actually do not want to happen. In fact the things that I actually hate happens to me or I find myself in certain situations that I know is rather ridiculous. But I manage to get out of them without getting involved with the law. I got the shock of my life as well when a bill came to me for about 345 guilders that I knew nothing about. Then I was being threatened in the name of the Queen, I paid the money and up to this moment I still don't know what it was for, and how it came to be.

In my old age I look back to when I was young. I am seeing every day how life rolls along. I see children going to school; people getting married; shops being opened; sports being played; people going to their work. But I'm not asking any questions why all these things are like that. That is what actually happens as we go through the three stages of life – early, middle and late.

I'm almost finishing a book by Ncholas Everitt entitled *The Non-existence of God*. I had to take my time and read it slowly. My English has become much better when I read these heavy books.

A strange thing happened to me a couple days ago. I got a plastic bag and it's jammed packed with stuff. Over my shoulder I got a fairly big travelling bag, in my left hand I got this small hand bag (not a woman's bag). I also have this white plastic bag filled with bananas, apples, oranges, pears and tomatoes. The bus was coming up to the place where I live when the white plastic back with all the fruits snapped and everything went on the floor and rolling away. I'm trying to collect them all and stuffed them in the other plastic bag that was already full. At the same time, I'm waving to the bus driver to wait a bit. In the Netherlands the buses are always on time. The bus drove away and brought me to the following stop where I got out, still in a state of panic. I was glad when I got home, sat down and relaxed. What has happened is recorded, but I'm not thinking about it, only when I have to talk about that day.

I like talking to old people wanting to know how they feel now and listen to stories of when they were young. Some of them are still on bicycles riding up and down like children.

Looking around me, I see the little children – boys and girls, running around, some only ten months old, and kicking football and carrying little shopping bags. Even already trying to get on their bicycles.

Remember that girl who I told you I met when I was at the station? I bumped into her again at the bus stop in the middle of the town. I said to her, "Are you a bossy woman?" She hesitated for a few seconds then said, "No, I'm not!" She said that she is a hairstylist.

I just picked up a new book called *Shadows of the Mind* by Roger Penrose. It is a very interesting book. I hope my mind doesn't blow after reading it...

No. My mind hasn't blown yet. I am still busy reading and enjoying it.

At the moment, I'm trying to understand certain things that has really baffled me. If a person tell me that they're religious, I respect them very much, and often listen to the reason why they became religious.

About six of us were sat at a table. There was a very young chap who said that he was a Christian. I know what that mean so I kept on drinking my beer; at that time I used to be a heavy drinker. I gave that up in 1978. Anyway, some of the other chaps started niggling him over the fact that he was a Christian. So I got to telling them leave the chap alone.

I am definitely not going to put myself in a situation where I turn out looking stupid. If I don't know anything about a subject, I'll keep my mouth shut; but if I know about it, and have read up on it, then it would be hard to shut me up.

There are some things of course that I cannot tell you over the internet. They are not bad or anything like that, only they're not to be told to Tom, Dick and Harry.

I have come to a final conclusion that the planets has something to do with our existence. I have been trying for many years to thrash this out. It doesn't of course appeal to many intellectuals.

I think that it is a wise thing to get your astrological chart done by a professional astrologer and be at peace with yourself.

I am not saying that astrology is all there is, what I'm saying is that it is *part* of our existence.

*

There are three things in my life that I have never done. They are:

1. I have never ever killed a human being, and I have no intention of doing so.

2. I have never ever told on or reported against my neighbour. That code almost got broken when a neighbour went too far; I kept my cool.

3. I have never ever tried to lead a married woman astray, or to be disrepectful to them.

These are three codes I hope I could keep until the planetary combinations says it is time for me to depart.

I'm like an observer looking at human beings and how they behave themselves. I have found it rather amazing how some human beings behave. You would think that they own the planet; but believe me, they have a lot to learn.

I have read so many stories about children who were under the care of their parents in poor conditions, and rose up in the end, to make something of themselves. These ones I have great respect for.

One of the stories that really got to me is that of Annie Oakley. I've read it so many times. Brought up in poor conditions, and at the time when women had no real say; she grew up and became a sharp shooter – an expert markswoman. She was the most famous show woman in America at the time. She paved the way for women athletes, and showed the men that women can shoot as well.

I do not like guns and all those things. But for competition shooting I can watch it.

I love watching tennis, it's beautiful to watch. I love watching football, I get a real kick from doing so. Sometimes I get upset when my team is losing. I do not go around smashing up things. When I use to drink, I'll go to the pub with friends and have a few.

There's no sport around that I wouldn't watch. I spent hours watching ski-ing, sailing, mountain climbing, cricket, badminton, racing, athletics, I did a lot of that myself. I love to watch cross-country, rugby, darts. When I was in the army, we did nothing else but playing darts and snooker which kept us happy.

A wise man knows that all things comes to an end. He does not fool himself or rush to the end before his time. He still try to do the things that he is still capable of doing. Was Solomon really that wise? He did disobey the command of God; but we are human beings, and we do and say foolish things.

9

Moving towards the end

Hello! Hello! I am here. It's been some time now since I last wrote something. Well, I'm still here and kicking. Still enjoying life, not thinking about the end, but it is creeping up slowly. The funny thing about life is that when we are young we just don't give a damn. We think we are it, that's what youth does to us. But in each generation the young will always find a way to enjoy themselves. As for me when I was young, I worked hard with good enjoyment. I think that the best time of my life was when I joined the Army. Anyone who has joined the army and enjoyed it would know what I mean.

I have been watching my planets in my astrological chart, and I am amazed. They want to put me in a love match. They want to make me a scientist. I should be a writer. The love match I think I could manage even though I'm reaching out for 80. I always love to read other people's books, but to write one, I didn't think I was that intellectual. My English isn't that good. I wish I had taken time to study it when I was young. I started collecting lots of books from the scientists. The subject I was interested in is that of *Time*. There's no one who knows what it is. I started thinking about it.

Astrology to me is like the sun, it is there and working. Only those who are interested will stop and study them. For me, many questions tumbled out from within me. Of course, the first one is that of 'free will.' I got around that by understanding that some things are fixed and human beings cannot do anything about it; like the natural laws. For years, I spent time doing lots of charts, and although I have a chart in front of me and looking at all the planets positions for an individual, I was still a bit baffled. But I was lucky to be around people who I associated with for a long time, and through that, I was able to see how the planets work, I still wasn't satisfied, for being a bit of a humanist, I didn't like the idea of things planned for us, like the planets. I could understand if your parents planned something for you or some club or organisation, that's different.

I tackled my own chart first, and found it to be true. Then I went around and collected material on the subject. Everyone has their own interpretation, so you can get yourself tangled up.

Then I understood the movement of the planets in my chart. The year I got married; the year I moved houses; the year my wife got her first daughter, and then the second. The year we parted. The year I met someone else and so forth. Does it all make any sense? Yes, it does.

It is worth getting a chart done for your children. You can see clearly how to guide them along; but still some of them have their own way according to what the planets are doing. An example is: as follows, if a child has the planet Venus at the top of their chart, that's a good sign to have lots of nice pretty things in their room, and nice music, for the child is bound to be interested in something to do with art or singing, it is also good for the career.

Guess what? I just talked about writing. My first book is being published. Then last year The sun and Uranus made contact with each other. This is the opportunity for me to dig in and understand a little about what the scientists are talking about. People with this connection turns out to be interested in science.

I had been thinking back when I was back home and the in thing at the time was collecting all those comic books. A lot of swapping went on. Then you had those who had families in America, so it was easy to get those comics over. You had to be careful because we used to take them to school and get in trouble with the teachers.

I like to dig into the bible now and then. Sometimes I get lost like when you are in a thick forest and do not know your way out. I read the book of *Job* many times. It is interesting because Job knew quite a lot, but when things went wrong for him he started cursing the day that he was born. Then his friends came to console him, and he would tell them off at times.

I feel strongly that there is a great power which I call the 'First Power Over All.' We are told that we must praise Him for what He has done; and I do that often. But I still see the road in front of me, and walk carefully upon it.

I like to have a peaceful way of life. I do not like war, but if some other would like to attack us, then even at my age, I won't just lie down and don't do anything. If I was afraid of dying, I would not have gone into the army. But it was good I did, I got lots of discipline to accompany what I had already gotten from my parents.

I know what poor mean. I experienced it, and I never asked any questions about it. I just did what I had to do. I like to see the place where I live, I mean in the town or the city,happiness and peace. That pleases me very much. I know that the world functions on positive and negative energies.

Sometimes I like starting a sentence with 'And' but I learned that it's not good to do so. I'm trying to cut it out.

Talking about 'Time' the scientist Sean Carrol is still trying to see if he could capture what it's all about. I had sore head from thinking about it. One time I pictured lots of strings dangling from a tree; and another time I pictured lots of dots all over the paper.

I don't mind people having any kind of dog that they like, but they must make sure that if the dogs are dangerous, they must keep them away from children. I am not talking about guard dogs. I have read many times about some pit bull dogs that have killed children – that I don't like.

I have to walk to the bus stop sometimes three times a week. There's a family who has a massive pit bull dog. Every time I pass, it is always snapping at me. One time I was standing at the bus stop when the woman came along with it. It came again at me, snapping away at the air, which could have been my legs. I think that if the woman wasn't strong enough to hold him back, it would have been feasting on my foot.

Remember I told you that I have the ability now to get into scientifical things? Well, I did, and I had to ease off for a while, it was heavy stuff. I still have two years in which the energies are there for me to understand it. I've been writing poems and some of them are quite unusual and scientific.

I like old people, for they have shown me that they're not old for nothing. They have made it through and they have lots of experience with them, some positive and some negative. I was going to the bus stop when this old dear of 77 years approached me and got interested in me. Every time I see her, I try to get away as quick as I can, trying not to show any bad feelings.

*

Wake up you young ones, and you old ones as well! I am still breathing and enjoying the life that has been created for us. I am still thinking a lot, and trying not to think a lot. It is rather difficult to switch off when you have so many things and people around you. Everything is in motion. Even when you are sitting still, the earth is still spinning around upon its journey. Do you know where it's going – I haven't a clue – and I don't think anyone knows.

Not so long ago, I was on the bus. I had my shoulder bag over my head and across my backso that it was now on my right side. Normally, I would have it over my right shoulder, and it would keep on falling off. On the bus I would have it on the floor with the straps over my right knee. This day, with it over my head and on the right side of me, I forgot all about it when I was on the bus. Sitting there, the bag was on the seat on my right, and I was half sitting on it. Suddenly after a few minutes, I looked down to my right knee, and didn't see the bag. I started panicking, could you imagine that feeling? Then I was relieved when I touched the straps across my back and chest.

A couple days ago, my book arrived from the publishers. What a great feeling that is. It's like a miracle. Seeing my name there in print. It is only a small one, but it's a start.

*

Hello all, I am still here enjoying what is left of my life. Quite a lot has happened. Nothing bad though. Well, except for a planet that was giving me trouble with backache, and at the same time giving me energies to dig into astronomy and scientifical things. If anyone of you knows anything about astrology, you would know that I am talking about the planet Uranus, I also had pain just below my right knee which is the calf. Uranus is also responsible for that area, ruled by Aquarius.

I am trying to halt my thinking, especially about how events come about. Now that Uranus is with me, I'm trying to see if I could get some insight.

In a vision, we can see the future and remember it, just like we remember past events. But if there's no visions of the future, then it cannot be remembered before it takes place.

We know that human beings has free will. They can do whatever they like, but the law is there to prevent them from going too far. Sometimes that doesn't even stop some of them.

If an astrologer had told me that I would get married in a certain year, I would not have believed him. So what caused that event to take place. We know that love feelings had something to do with it; and being attracted to someone very strongly. But is there something *else*?

I believe strongly that there is something else. It is a pity that some of our scientists has failed to see the workings of astrology. I would like to declare that it is a science but I am not a scientist, and have no power to do so. From my ownself, I say that astrology is a science, and is very helpful when it is properly used.

I was in London in 2004, and a woman told me the exact year when I shall not be around. But I'm the type of person I do not think about such things. They just happen.

Hello there, again! I am still around but God knows for how long. That's not my problem. I am not the Creator who knows more than I.

*

Quite a lot has happened since I last wrote something down. My friend who is married, a nice blue-eyed woman has taken some of my books into the shop where she works, it's a book shop. And my second book is about to be started. If the publisher likes it, then he'll publish it.

It's gone a very long time since the buses here been on strike. Well, I was at the bus stop waiting for the bus that didn't come. I had to get myself a taxi to the town and back. That day it cost me quite a lot. But now everything is back to normal.

Yes, I'm still here batting every day as if I'm in a cricket match, and I'm the last batsman to try and make the runs that our team is aiming for.

10

Still hanging on

Wake up all you young ones and look life straight into its face. See the positives and the negatives, and do something about it. You old ones, carry on as if you're not going to depart. At least you've had your run.

Quite a lot has happened, and I just don't know where to start. Okay, let me start with some good news: I reached my 76th birthday, and I'm still kicking. I know that there are people who reached over a 100, but I do not think about my age, nor do I think about tomorrow. I would only think about tomorrow if I had something planned, like going on holidays with the family or something like that. Or you have some appointment to meet.

My second book is published, and the third is now with the publishers. I'm getting in the swing of writing many short stories, most I do just for a laugh and a challenge. I think that if I was very good with English language, I would have been writing in another way, but I prefer this way, it is simple, and I hope my readers understand me. I don't want to write so that my readers are baffled.

A couple months ago, I got an invitation from the High School where I worked for 16 years. A woman there was leaving after working for 45 years. I knew her, and we got on well together, she was married and had two grown up boys. I decided to go and did so. The funny thing was, I hadn't been in that part for at least 11 years, and believe it or not, I didn't know where the school was.

It's an area where many different schools are there together. I got on the bus, which was a special bus for the students, stayed on the bus which was packed tightly. The bus made its round and I found myself back at the bus station. I got off the bus, making my way to where I could catch another bus. Who do you think I bumped into? Yes, that girl I told you about who met me some time ago.

I don't know what it is, but I keep bumping into this girl. She's very nice and spontaneous, always with this smile on her face. She keeps telling me that I should call her.

At my age, quite a lot of things are happening. And suddenly, my Moon is passing through Cancer, which mean changes. Then a whopping sun opposing Uranus. This does not happen often. And Uranus, being a sudden and unusual and disrupted planet, will definitely upset things.

But I had my eyes on it for some time now. I don't normally look at my chart. But I am glad I did. I could have been in more trouble had I gotten angry and lashed out stupidly. But I took everything calmly.

*

Hello, I am here, still breathing the breath of life. God knows for how long. But I will not hesitate, and carry on doing what I like to, researching and writing poems.

A lot has happened since I last wrote something here. I will start with what I had been telling you about my sun opposing Uranus.

It was like going through hell – if there is such a place – and still managed to come out unscathed. *Phew!* What an experience that was. I would not like to go through it again. But I got to know quite a lot about some scientifical things that I never knew before. Very intellectual – you'd think that I was a scientist – and at the same time, I was holding back, not going too deep in.

Also by John Gumbs

Jehanne 978-1-78222-571-3
The Trial and Burning of Jehanne 978-1-78222-609-3
Aitch H 978-1-78222-628-4
Jay G 978-1-78222-656-7
Heidi 978-1-78222-682-6
Sheila 978-1-78222-729-8

JEHANNE

John Gumbs

THE TRIAL AND BURNING OF
JEHANNE

John Gumbs

AITCH

Jay
G

John Gumbs

Heidi

John Gumbs

Sheila

John Gumbs

www.ingramcontent.com/pod-product-compliance
Lightning Source LLC
Chambersburg PA
CBHW071318130626
46556CB00004B/1648